KAT ADDAMS

I don't know where I'm going from here,
but I promise it won't be boring.

—David Bowie

HAILEY

I pushed my way through the crowded room toward the corner in the back. In the Delta Iota Kappa house—or the DIK house, as my sorority sisters and I called it—the back corner was reserved for only special people, like me.

"Hey, babe!"

A sloppy-drunk student reached out to grab my arm and pull me toward him, but I dug my designer heel into his toe and pushed him away. I didn't have time for riffraff. I was on a mission tonight. The stench of beer, pot, and college hormones stifled my breathing as I fought my way through the crowd. I gripped my drink with one hand and my boujee clutch in the other, like a snooty fashionista—a telltale sign of the Beta Alpha Delta, or BAD, sisters. We could attend a swamp party in the festering heat of Louisiana and still dress to kill. I knew. I'd done it.

"There you are! I thought you might have gotten lost. Or distracted by a DIK-head. Look," Madison, my best friend and president of my sorority house, shouted over the music.

She nudged me with her pointed elbow and nodded toward the stairwell. Three of the hopefuls we'd picked for this rush mission were canoodling with the local frat boys, inching their way up the stairs and toward their goal.

"I think they'll make it. I told Diana if she so much as spilled an ounce of mud in her Birkin bag, she's out." Madison pretended to sip her drink. We always pretended.

I touched the rim of the cup to my mouth, tipped it back until I felt the warm, stale beer hit my lips, and then stopped.

Rule number two in the BAD house: we didn't drink at parties unless they were events.

A frat party sure as hell didn't count as an event.

BAD members always needed to be poised and on our toes. We had to represent our house in the most polished and fashionable light. After all, we were the only fashion academy sorority across the entire southeastern region. We had a lot of eyes on us. The last thing we needed was a scandalous photo gracing our social media pages. We couldn't get shit-faced on cheap beer and tequila. Not in public anyway. Our reputations were always in the spotlight.

"Why would you let her use a Birkin bag for a mission like this? We could have given her a knockoff." My eyes followed the girls up the stairs until they disappeared.

The frat boys swayed, stumbling along behind them, snickering and hiccuping in a fit of drunk hope.

"It's Diana Marshall. Her parents own banks. She probably has eight more in her closet." She tucked a long white strand of hair behind her ear and smirked. Her lone dimple winked at me.

"Still, that's disrespectful to the bag!" I shook my head.

My family had plenty of money, but we were still no match for the richest of the rich in Forks. The way Madison and most of my friends blew through cash never ceased to amaze me. They never bothered to look at price tags or check their bank accounts. Their credit card limits were endless, and their parents footed the bills without question.

I wasn't that lucky or irresponsible. I only owned one credit card, and I even occasionally paid it with the money from my bank account, which, admittedly, was funded by my dear old dad. I couldn't help it if I was a spoiled only child. My family did well, but we weren't at the top of the food chain—unlike Madison. I drove an Audi instead of a Jaguar, and my closet was only half as full as the other sisters.

"What did you want me to do? Send her up there with a plastic Target bag full of mud? That's not obvious! Besides, if she wants to be a sister, she'll have to play the part. We all make sacrifices in one way or another," she said, stepping further back into the corner and snapping a selfie.

I'd noticed a handful of prestigious names mingling around us, but there were more than a few students I'd never seen before.

"Oh yeah? What sacrifices have you made?" I grinned, pretending to sip my drink again.

"Guiding these little shits like this. Making their poor souls perform stunts and grovel at our feet. Breaks my heart." Madison touched her collar and sighed, shifting her weight to one foot in her signature pose.

She stood long-legged in an outfit tailored just for her. Her shorts lay low, slung over her bony hips, accentuating her tiny waist. She looked like a drawing, like the waif silhouettes I sketched in the studio. Her body, beauty, and attitude were almost impossible standards. No one could measure up to Madison Sheffield—except maybe me. I wasn't as rough around the edges as my best friend, but they didn't call us the BAD twins for nothing.

"You love it." I rolled my eyes and stuck my leg out, aware of all the attention on us.

Men watched us. Women watched us. Hell, if I had a mirror, I'd watch us work the crowd too.

"I do." A devilish grin spread across her face before she touched the cup to her lips and peered through the crowd, searching for the real reason she had come here tonight.

If looks could kill, Preston Lancaster would be lying in a pool of his own blood. Madison had had it out for him since I'd known her. Our first year at FU, she'd recounted the tales about how her brother's best friend had pestered her, growing up. He'd played tricks on Madison, humiliating her in front of the entire school.

"You aren't mad, are ya, Maddy?" he'd say.

The words would strike like venom.

Madison wasn't mad. She was livid. She'd been planning vengeance on him for years.

"Shit. My phone's buzzing. I bet it's the girls up there," she said, turning around and searching for a place to set her cup.

A dark-haired man sat alone on the couch behind us. He scanned the room, observing the crowd and, no doubt, making judgments. We all did it. I noticed his perfectly chiseled cheekbones before seeing his on-point leather jacket, which said a lot for me. I knew I wasn't supposed to judge a book by its cover, but fashion was my life. I had to take wardrobe choice into account.

I was a key sister in BAD—the most popular sorority at Fork University. Beauty. Aesthetics. Design. That was the Beta Alpha Delta way. B-A-D. I'd heard all the jokes. We were BAD bitches, Bitches At Design, Babes Are Dangerous, and I'd even once heard, Bitches Ate Dicks. That latter slogan didn't make sense unless they were talking about Cheri, our resident cam girl. But her secret was safe—supposedly. Only her besties, Madison and me, knew about her side hustle, and we'd remain loyal to the end.

I preferred to think of us BAD members as BADasses. We were committed to our education, lifestyle, goals, and each other. We never let anyone get in our way, especially a man—which was rule number one: besties before testes.

I side-eyed the man in the leather jacket. His lips parted, displaying a dazzling white set of veneers, just like mine.

He had classically handsome features—a rugged jawline, dark and mysterious eyes, and shoulders so broad that I'd have trouble peering over them while he banged away on top of me. He was a cliché. Basic. Vanilla. Again, just like me. Except he was more. At least much more than the sorry excuse of a boyfriend I had, who was probably sitting in front of a video game or jerking off to porn at his apartment.

Madison rudely reached across sexy leather-jacket man, setting her cup on the table and paying him no attention. I had no idea how she hadn't noticed him. All the money in the world couldn't buy a face like that in Forks' social circles. His nose alone sat perfectly poised on his face, as if he'd had it made into exactly the right size and placed in exactly the right spot. I'd never thought I would think a nose was sexy, but I'd nibble Mr. Leather Jacket's nose.

He leaned back from Madison's reach, narrowly avoiding her drink. I caught his gaze and tried to raise my eyebrows in apology, but his eyes shifted to my exposed midriff. When the bare-belly trend had come back in style, I'd furiously hit the gym. And by furiously, I meant, I had done a few sit-ups and checked out the local beefcakes between selfies.

"Fuck," I muttered, swiveling around so my back was to him again. A rush of heat flushed through me, settling in my cheeks.

"What?" Madison fished her phone out of her bag and read her texts. Her face froze, like the one time she'd pressured the aesthetician into giving her way too much Botox. Her eyebrows had stayed near her hairline for months. "Time to go. Code red."

She pulled me away. My beer fell, sloshing out of my cup and barely missing my designer heels.

The three BAD recruits ran down the stairs. The frat boys followed closely behind, drunkenly stumbling after them. Under one of the man's arms was Sanchez the mutt, the DIK house mascot. Both the man and the dog dripped with mud, but Sanchez didn't seem to mind. He was tucked snugly under the armpit of the frat boy. Between the dog's tiny teeth was the giant bone we'd bought him for his participation in our prank. With each bobble and shake down the stairs, Sanchez never dropped the treat.

"We've been infiltrated!" one of the boys slurred, shouting above the music.

The DIKs prickled, searching around the room, but the rest of the partygoers continued drinking and mingling as if it were just another typical day at the frat house.

Diana flew past me, heels in hand, laughing like a maniac. I sighed at her Birkin bag, caked with mud. The other two recruits ran behind her, quickly followed by Madison and me. I could see a disaster before it happened, not because I was psychic or anything, but because I'd been through enough shenanigans with Madison to know trouble when it came knocking.

"Go, go, go!" I shooed them toward the door and fought through the crowd again.

My heart raced, thumping in my ears as I held on to the back of Madison's tailored blouse. She pushed her way through everyone, stepping on toes, elbowing abs, and barking orders for people to get out of the way. The crowd parted for Madison without hesitation, and that was where our similarities stopped. I was a much more reserved sister and typically preferred my fashion choices to do my talking. Madison, not so much. If she were in the general vicinity, you'd know it.

We made it to the front door before the rest of the DIK brothers sobered enough to understand the situation.

"Who did this? Who gave us a dirty Sanchez?" Preston cried, grabbing the tiny dog and holding him up for all to see.

Sanchez still held his bone in what I could only describe as a toothy grin. I didn't feel wrong about muddying up the poor mutt. Dogs liked getting dirty. And besides, we had given him a massive treat for his cooperation. It could have been much worse. We could have set fire to the house. I was pretty sure Madison wouldn't have turned down that idea.

"You aren't mad, are ya?" Madison shouted back before slipping off her heels and running away, roaring with laughter.

I tugged at my brand-new pumps, prying them off and clutching them to my chest with my bag. I pushed my heels into the ground and ran like my life depended on it. I didn't want a muddy dog—or worse, Preston—anywhere near my Louis Vuitton. I huffed out shaky breaths through lungs burning like fire and cursed myself for not truly working out at the gym and fucking off instead.

All those countless hours spent strutting in front of the gym bros, I'd wasted. I could have had washboard abs and buns of steel by now. But my body was built on a solid foundation of caffeine and French pastries à la the couture life. The only thing missing from my image was a long, thin cigarette poking from between my lips.

Up ahead, Madison shouted into her phone.

"Cheri, bring the car around. Code red. Diana and two others are ahead of me. We're coming to you. Start her up." She bolted off, hurtling this way and that and leaving me behind in her dust.

Unlike me, Madison actually did exercise at the gym. She took Pilates and spin, and she could contort her body in several different yoga positions. Drunk Madison loved to show off her flexible talents before falling over and snorting until she hiccuped herself to sleep.

I heaved, pushing my heels into the ground harder and running across the expansive yards on Greek Row. I hopped over the exposed roots of trees, a discarded red Solo cup, and a Birkin bag.

A Birkin bag?

Diana's mud-stained bag lay in the wet grass with the contents strewn all over the place. I stooped to pick it up as

I ran past it, but a hand reached out from behind me, swooping me into an embrace. I could tell from the heavy leather scent of his jacket that the man back at the party had caught me. I shrieked, but Madison and the girls were too far ahead to hear.

"What're you doing? Put me down!" I hit him in the chest with the Birkin bag while still holding my shoes and clutch with the other. I couldn't lose my designer labels. A girl had priorities!

"Calm down, damn it. I'm saving you. You don't have any idea what you're playing at." He took off in a run, following my sisters.

I curled into him, cradling my belongings in my lap, and shot him a skeptical glance. For a second—a very slight second—I lay my head against his chest and pretended this was romantic and not weird at all. This hot guy was my hero, saving me and my precious wardrobe from a fire—like the dumpster fire that was my life. I snapped myself out of my fantasy as he leaped through the air, barely winded, even while holding me. Again, I beat myself up for not working out at the gym and hashtagging lies like I had. He probably felt like he was carrying a sack of potatoes in his ridiculously strong arms.

"Why are you saving me?"

"Because my brothers aren't going to be nice when they catch you. They've been hazing recruits all week. They're riled up for fresh meat, and you, you're as fresh as they come. They'd love to get ahold of you and your bubblegum-pink hair. Maybe I would too," he growled, holding me tight against him. "Such a BAD girl. I've heard stories about you ladies, but I had no idea. The dirty Sanchez prank was all sorts of wrong. But also, pretty damn funny. I'll give you that. Except … that poor dog." He clicked his tongue, chastising me.

"Yeah, yeah. We gave him a bone! It's not like we gave him a bad haircut. We just let him roll in the mud a bit. Like a normal dog," I huffed, still trying to catch my breath from my run.

"I see. So, normal dog things. Unlike the stuff they put him through, like dressing him up in bow ties and feeding him lamb chops out of a golden bowl. What's worse than a dirty Sanchez? A pussy Sanchez. They should let him be a dog." He crushed me into his chest and jumped over a sprinkler, narrowly missing a soaked butt.

I shifted further into him. My nipples stiffened against his rock-hard pecs. I'd always wondered how a muscled-up man felt. I longed to run my palms along every line of his six-pack abs, bulging biceps, and a back that felt like carved marble. But that wouldn't happen with my boyfriend. Joel was soft and pudgy like an overripe avocado. I'd once sat on his lap and melted into him. I'd somehow left butt imprints on his memory-foam thighs. I hadn't had the opportunity to play with much else on this new man's body, but I could get used to his ripples. He felt exactly how I'd imagined—irresistible.

"Didn't know a DIK would care so much about animal welfare—or my welfare actually. I can't believe you're one of them. I've never seen you before. You seem less … DIK-ish." I reached up, tracing the five o'clock shadow of his jawline before realizing what I was doing.

He glanced down, flashing those pearly whites before slowing to a stop. "Just wait."

He set me down behind a tree, pushed me up against it, and pressed his lips hard on mine before I could resist. I wouldn't have resisted anyway. I mean, sure, there was the douche-bag man of mine who I stubbornly called my boyfriend. But I pretended with him, just like I did with everything else. My love for him wasn't real, and this shenanigan wasn't either. This was just a friendly kiss to thank my hero for saving me. He entwined his fingers with mine, clutching my hands and pinning them up over my head against the rough bark. His tongue slipped over my lips, and for a moment, I forgot to breathe.

"Dominick!" a familiar voice shouted behind us. "Which way did they go?"

"Damn it," he whispered, pulling away. He pressed his finger to my lips before stepping out from behind the tree. "I don't know, Preston. I think they got us this time. They ran, and I couldn't keep up. We'll get them back. Let's go clean up poor Sanchez. Then, we can think straight and plot our next move." Dominick's voice trailed off as they made their way back.

I peeked out from around the tree, making sure they had both left before I tiptoed to the car driving toward me. I knew it was my sisters. The Hummer Cheri's dad had bought her wasn't exactly stealthy.

"Shit! I thought someone had gotten you! What happened? Your makeup is smeared all over your face! Did you fall? Are you hurt?" Madison cried as I opened the door and hopped inside.

"Yep. I tripped. Rough fall. But I saved the bag!" I held up Diana's Birkin bag.

I didn't want to tell Madison about my sexy hero in front of the other girls. Besides, once she found out he was a DIK, she would probably flip her shit. Even though she begged me to get rid of my dickhead boyfriend, I somehow doubted she wanted to see me with a member of her mortal enemy's fraternity.

"Oh, Hailey. That's just like you." Madison laughed. "To the house, please, Cheri! But first, creep past the DIK house. I want to see if we ruined their party."

"Ten-four." Cheri swerved the Hummer around.

Diana and the recruits cackled as they recounted their endeavors to us. I nodded, pretending to listen, but my eyes were on the two men walking back toward the party. Even the way Dominick sauntered down the sidewalk sent a rush of heat between my legs.

"Shh. Look. There's the loser now." Madison jerked her head to Preston.

"Why is he with Dominick Moretti?" Diana asked, leaning across me to get a better look. "I thought he was too good to go to Forks University. What's he doing back home?"

"Wait. Who did you just say?" I glanced at Madison, who shook her head not so subtly at Diana.

"Oh. I, um ... just some guy." Diana cringed, shrugging her shoulders.

"No. Not just some guy. You said, Dominick Moretti. As in Moretti Hotels?" My pulse weakened. I put my hand on my chest, pushing it in and forcing myself to breathe, as if I had to give myself CPR. I didn't know the first thing about CPR, but I'd gone through a weird *Baywatch* marathon phase a few years back and figured I could resuscitate someone if I needed to.

Madison sighed from the front. "Yes. He's Louis Moretti's son. I don't know what happened, but he's a student at FU now and also a DIK. Obviously. I should have told you all, but we don't talk about the Morettis in the BAD house—new rule. Let's forget we ever saw him."

The girls nodded.

Right. Forget.

I slumped back in my seat. Like Madison and her mortal enemy, I had one too. The Morettis and my family, the Simmons, had been at battle for as long as I could remember. Our fathers had been best friends once. Inseparable, was how I'd heard the story—like a bromance similar to Preston and Madison's brother. But Louis Moretti took business plans he and my dad had worked on together and ran with it, stealing them and business—i.e., money—from my family. The Morettis had flourished, and we had struggled.

In the end, we still did okay, even more than okay for most people. I wasn't hurting for anything. But I knew never to mention the name Moretti to my parents. Saying that surname aloud was worse than uttering a four-letter curse word in my conservative home.

Dominick looked up and into our tinted windows as we slowly crept past them.

"Good job on the dirty Sanchez, ladies. Let's go home. I'm exhausted!" I sighed. My stomach twisted into a knot as I swallowed hard and pretended that whatever crazy fiasco had just happened to me hadn't.

Sunday mornings were usually reserved for BAD brunch, but today, Madison and I were too busy to relax and drink mimosas. So, instead, we worked and drank mimosas. Our annual charity Christmas fashion show was coming up, and since all of our focus had been on the recruits, we hadn't even begun to plan this year's event.

I washed my face in the sink and stared into the mirror, pulling my bubblegum-pink hair into a messy bun. My hair wasn't only a calculated fashion choice, but also a loud statement. To get ahead in my school, I needed to stand out, and unfortunately for me, I was as basic as they came. I liked my pumpkin spice lattes with an oversize hoodie. I knew the lyrics to almost every John Mayer song. My social media pages were full of selfies with the occasional motivational quote thrown in for variety. My fashion icon was Kate Middleton, and my me time was spent getting manis and pedis while rocking out with my AirPods and hashtagging my vibes. I was one hundred percent that basic bitch. My pink hair was the wildest choice I'd ever made—until last night.

"Dominick Moretti," I whispered to my reflection.

The way he had tasted on my lips left anything but a bad taste in my mouth.

I'd heard rumors before about the Morettis' son. But since he'd attended the most prestigious prep school in Forks and then flown off to an Ivy League college, I'd never known him. He wasn't a part of my social circle, and I was undoubtedly too low on his list. His incredibly fit stature told me his type was probably the bubble-butt girls in the gym—not the bubblegum girls at the fashion academy. A man like him had options, so why the hell he'd kissed me, I didn't know.

I'd always pictured Louis's son to be the spitting image of his dad—short, dumpy, little hands. He wasn't any of those things. The only similar trait I could see in what I knew about the two would be their apparent ability to do whatever the fuck they wanted and think about the consequences later—or not at all.

In Dominick's case, he didn't have any consequences. Sure, I could have told him to stop kissing me because who the hell did he think he was? Dominick Moretti—that was who. And I hadn't wanted him to stop kissing me, not even if I had known it was him. It felt … good. Freeing. After all, I was a basic bitch in need of something or someone to bring me out of my vanilla tendencies. Life had been unfulfilling lately. There wasn't any harm in a simple, unprovoked kiss—not from him anyway.

I sighed, checking my phone for a text from my boyfriend. Joel was another basic-bitch symptom. He was a lazy, mouthy pothead, coasting through school on his family's money. He didn't care about anything, except video games, porn, Discord—whatever the hell that was— drinking beer, and shooting the shit with his other loser friends. We'd been together just over a year now, and while we did sometimes do things together, we mostly didn't. I had no idea why we kept each other around. I chalked it up to my basic-bitch tendencies of playing it safe. And from his side, I was sure he kept me around because I made him look good.

"What's taking so long?" Madison called from the other side of the bathroom door. "You haven't had your coffee yet, so I know you're not on the toilet! Now, get out here and help me with these youngins!"

"Rude! Go back to your own bathroom! I didn't work my way into my third year to share my space. I need peace in the morning. Especially before my coffee." I swung open the door and stared back at Madison.

Her long, blindingly stark white hair hung in two braids trailing down either side of her shoulders. Her black silken robe was tied across her starched leopard-print pajamas— all matchy-matchy. But Madison was anything but basic. She set trends every season, invented an iconic brand she planned on growing into a business, and turned heads wherever she went. The world was her runway, and she ran all over it.

Of course, she'd had the advantage of growing up in the industry. Her mom was president of the fashion academy and a very well-known cougar at FU. Boys didn't often grace our building, but when they did, Ms. Liza Sheffield—thrice-divorced—was ready to pounce, much to her daughter's dismay.

Ms. Sheffield had been a part of the elite ever since her first husband, whom she divorced and took to the cleaners. The literal cleaners. They'd owned a dry-cleaning business that was franchised over the entire southeastern region and Texas.

Once she had a nice divorce settlement, she invested in the fashion academy, following her dream and becoming a vital member of the university. She'd built our sorority from the ground up, implemented a few new courses at the academy, and funded the annual fashion show charity— which, of course, her daughter, Madison, now headed. Money talked, and FU didn't argue. Besides, everyone liked the Sheffields. They were the rare type of wealthy who spread it. They gave back to the community and invested in several local charities. Their too-hot-to-handle attitude could easily be overlooked for the good deeds they did.

I grabbed my phone and pushed past Madison, catching a whiff of her signature scent—plum, spice, and a cutting edge of dark cherry that made my mouth pucker. She'd mixed the perfumes herself—just another one of her many talents.

"Let me guess. You're in here, texting Joel. Oh, wait. No, you're not because he never texts you. You're just waiting on him. Honestly, Hailey, please just dump that man-child. He holds you back. Why would you be up here, texting a man you don't love and have no feelings for, instead of coming downstairs to help me with our bright futures?" Madison followed behind me.

I had no idea how she had so much energy in the morning. She was my best friend, but it had taken me a very long time to handle her in large doses.

"Who says I have no feelings for Joel?" I marched toward the back deck, where catering set up our brunch every Sunday—another perk from Ms. Liza Moneybags.

She spoiled Madison and her sorority sisters. But I wasn't complaining. Before becoming a sorority sister, I'd never eaten ceviche for breakfast—or ever.

"You. Don't you remember? Ugh. You have to lay off the wine on girls' night if you can't even remember what you're saying or doing. But hey! Truth comes out when you're drinking at least. Let's see ... you said you had no feelings for your boyfriend but were keeping him around just because. You thought *Friends* was the dumbest show on the planet. I'm still hurt over that, by the way. It's a cult classic! Jeez. Oh, and you mentioned some new vibrator you'd bought that made you drool a little and cross your eyes. I still need you to send me the link for it."

"Damn it. Don't let me drink an entire bottle next time. Who else heard my confessional?"

"Just Cheri. Everyone else had gone to bed. No worries. Your secrets are safe with us. But you need to dump that piece of shit. The world is our oyster. Scratch that. It's our caviar. We're moving up and on as boss babes. We'll have our pick of men from high society. Or low. Whatever floats your boat. Personally, I'm shooting high. Not as high as me.

That might hurt my ego. But high nonetheless. And not high as in a lazy stoner like yours."

I paused before opening the door to the patio. I needed a breather. I had only been up for a few minutes, and Madison was already exhausting me. I mentally checked my calendar to see if I could catch a nap today.

"Can we not talk about Joel? Let's just work. Besides, I don't want anyone else out here in my business. I know they're my sisters, but I don't trust anyone, except you and Cheri."

"You don't trust us, or you're ashamed of Joel and you don't want him mentioned because he's an embarrassment to you and society?"

"Fuck, Madison. I need coffee before you. We can continue this convo later. I'm still recovering from last night. How are you so charged up? All the anxiety and suspense were draining. What if one of us had gotten caught? By Preston … or worse … Dominick Moretti." I flinched after saying the name aloud while doing my best to pry information out of my best friend.

She sighed, walking around me and opening the door. We made our way toward the buffet and past two half-empty tables. It was still too early on a Sunday for everyone to be awake and as lively as Madison.

"You stopped talking," I whispered. "You wouldn't shut up a second ago. So, you knew he was here, and I'm betting you knew he was a DIK. So, tell me, why didn't you warn me? You could have at least told me who to look out for. His family—"

"I thought if I ignored it all, then you'd never know. I didn't think you would find out or that someone would stupidly point out a Moretti to you or any Simmons, and vice versa. Everyone in this damn town knows the drama between your families. I'd heard he was back a while ago. He was naturally a shoo-in for DIK. Money talks. You know it. I know it. If it makes a difference, I don't think he's like his family. I mean, I don't know the guy, but I've heard rumors that he's not so bad."

"You knew Dominick Moretti sat right behind us in the corner last night, and you didn't even warn me." I clenched my jaw, eyeballing the stack of French pastries on the buffet.

"Yes. And I'm guessing he knew who you were, too, because he couldn't stop staring. I even tried to block his view a few times, but his eyes stayed fixed on you. I thought if you didn't know, it would be for the best. Then, he'd think you were acting like he didn't exist. Just think about it. If you knew Dominick Moretti was in the DIK house last night, you wouldn't have set foot in that party with me. You can't let his family rule you, as your dad did." She handed me a plate. "I'm sorry I didn't fess up, Hailey. I thought I was doing the right thing and hoped you'd never find out about him. But now, you know who he is and can avoid him. I should have told you. I just didn't want to bring up drama. Surprisingly, because I live for that shit." She laughed.

"Thanks for trying to protect me, I guess. But next time, I'm pretty sure I can handle it. I handle you." I raised my eyebrows while heavy-handing the champagne for my mimosa.

"Touché," Madison sighed, inspecting her perfectly manicured nails.

DOMINICK

"Stay on your toes," Preston warned me before completely ignoring his own advice and performing his signature booty-popping on a keg-stand trick.

He'd told me our fraternity was ripe for pranks tonight because, after all, we were DIKs.

When I'd applied to FU's veterinarian program, against my father's wishes, my dad had gestured wildly with his hands, overexaggerating in his old Italian ways, and thrown a man-child fit. I was his only child, and he wanted me to carry on the family architectural business. But I didn't want to build shit like my dad. Or worse, tear it down. I wanted to save shit. Like animals. Little, cute ones and big, ugly ones.

I was a lover of all creatures. My dad never understood that side of me, but my mom could stop his childish rants with the snap of her death stare. And that was how the conversation had ended, and I had begun my life back at home in Forks, attending my dream vet school under one condition from dear old dad—I had to become a DIK. He'd said I had to join the Delta Iota Kappa fraternity, or my funds for school were kaput. I hadn't argued.

I'd never considered myself the fraternity type. After watching my family canoodle with Forks' elite, the only thing I'd learned from these trust-fund kids and their parents was to watch my back. People with money couldn't be trusted, and I was one of those people. Or at least, my family was. I tried hard to scrub myself of the Moretti name and show people a different side of us, but it was useless. My dad had set our reputation in stone, and because of our Italian heritage and his incessant joking about the mob, no one really got close enough to get to know us anyway.

That hadn't bothered me so much. I was a loner and an introvert through and through. Give me my dog and my hiking boots, and I was as happy as could be. I didn't need to surround myself with friends, fake or not, and I'd surely never pictured myself as an infamous DIK. I hadn't even needed to participate in rush week or file an application. My father had thrown enough money at the fraternity that they gladly accepted me with open arms—just another day as a spoiled, little rich kid. But I wasn't spoiled, and I hated preconceived notions about me because of my massive trust fund.

"Did you see her come in a few minutes ago?" Preston asked. The stale beer on his breath nearly knocked me backward.

"See who?" I peered over the crowd, searching for I didn't know what.

"Hailey!"

"Who's Hailey?"

"Simmons! Hailey Simmons. Where have you been, man? She's Madison's best friend. The BAD girls. Remember I told you about them?" Preston groaned, putting his head in his hands and rubbing his eyes.

"Hailey Simmons is here? Where?" I gulped.

I hadn't seen a Simmons in ages, and I didn't want to. What I knew of the drama my dad had caused Hailey's family was despicable. Yet again, just another day in the elite crowd. Kill or be killed. Eat or get eaten. No matter how many charity events our social circle attended or how many pockets they lined for a "good cause," corruption lingered just beneath the surface. Or in the case of my family's feud with the Simmons, out in the open for all to see.

"She's the one with the pink hair! And Madison is the granny-white bleached-out babe in the corner over there. They look like two pastel anime characters dressed for their runway debut. How can you miss them?" Preston said. "Watch them. Go over there to Madison's corner and sit and observe. They'll be up to something, if I know Madison. She's a vengeful little brat. And I'm sure birds of a feather flock together. Hailey probably has it out for you because … ya know, you kinda fucked her."

"I didn't fuck her! My dad did!" I huffed a little too loudly.

The two couples standing beside us scooted away.

"Bro, that's even a bit much for me. And I'm kinky as fuck." Preston shoved his shoulder into mine, laughing.

"You know what I mean. I'm not my family. But I'll be on the lookout for trouble," I muttered.

"I knew you were a natural DIK. We're going to make a great team this year. I got your back. You got mine. I'll introduce you to the important people. Get you caught up to snuff. You're already quite the popular newcomer. If I wasn't so damn devilishly handsome myself, I might be a bit jealous. But I'm not. This is just the beginning of a beautiful bromance. After all, I need someone on my level to help me with these new bastards. Look at them out there, drowning in pussy. They can't even swim. They look like those baby seals flopping around, all confused and shit, before the killer whale gulps them down in one bite." He nodded toward a few recruits drunkenly dancing around three beautiful women, who were entirely out of their league.

"That's an insult to baby seals, but I see what you're saying. They need guidance. I know a lost cause when I see one. They're not getting anywhere tonight." A hint of smugness escaped my lips.

Back at Welshire, the school I'd attended before FU, I'd had my fair share of women. I never had anything lasting, but I wasn't exactly looking for love either. If I wanted a woman in my bed, I'd have one. If I didn't want to get laid, I wouldn't. I knew my way around a woman's body and bed. I didn't need help in that area like these clueless boys running around with their dicks practically hanging out, begging for attention.

"Exactly. And by the way, those women are dressed like they all share the same closet, so I'd say they were BAD. Those are the toughest nuts to crack. They'll crack our recruits' nuts instead. Just watch and see. Ugh. We have so much work to do." Preston shook his head.

Another brother shouted to him from across the room, and off he went, toward the keg.

I made my way to the back and settled on a couch right behind Madison. I sat back, straightening my jacket and waiting. I'd forgotten about being on the lookout for shenanigans the second Preston uttered her name—Hailey Simmons. My mission tonight was no longer to pledge allegiance to DIK, guarding whatever shit went down. My only mission was to find her. After that, I had no idea what I'd do.

The last time I'd seen Hailey was at the Tower Club when I was fifteen. Our families had both attended an event there, and after my father quickly pointed out the Simmons, they'd vanished before I could get a good look. The only thing I remembered about her was how she had sat, face turned down, pushing her fork around on her plate. She had looked just as bored and out of place as me.

"There you are! I thought you might have gotten lost. Or distracted by a DIK-head. Look," Madison said to the stunning woman who appeared next to her.

Hailey.

If Preston hadn't mentioned the bubblegum-pink hair, I never would have known it was her. Hailey didn't look anything like the young girl I had seen back at the Tower Club. She stood with her shoulders back, peering over everyone's head and not even giving me a second glance. I doubted she even noticed me or anyone other than herself. How could she? Hailey even outshone her friend, Madison, and that wasn't easy.

I slowed my breathing, aware of how high my heart rate had jumped the moment she came into my view. I lost myself in her beauty as I watched her animated conversation with Madison. I hadn't expected a Simmons to take my breath away, but here we were. My family's mortal enemy stood before me, wrapped in an air of confidence and dressed to kill. If she turned around and took one look at me ...

Fuck! There it is! She saw me!

I dodged Madison's drink as she reached across me and placed it on a table. Hailey turned her head and watched, locking her eyes on mine. I trailed my gaze down her taut body. I couldn't help it. The subtle sneak peek of bare skin just under her rib cage snapped me out of my trance. Her mouth turned down before she whirled back around.

I was done for. Hailey knew the creepy man sitting behind her was the heir to the Morettis' dirty money, stolen straight from her father's pockets. I didn't know the whole story about what had happened. My father refused to talk about it, and my mother always opened a bottle of wine the second the Simmons were mentioned. But I knew enough to determine my family had done hers wrong, and there was never an attempt at an apology or to make amends.

I took a deep breath. If my family wasn't brave enough to admit their faults and move on, I would have to do it myself. I bit my lip, gathering the courage to introduce myself. I went over the different scenarios in my head of how she'd react.

Would she hit me with her bag?
Would she slap me across the face?
Would she throw that beer she pretended to drink in my eyes?
Or worse, would she ignore me?

Clearly, if she knew who I was and turned her back on me, she didn't want anything to do with me. I couldn't blame her. Nothing good could come of us befriending each other. Our families would probably kick us both out of FU and cut us from our trust funds if we so much as talked about the weather. I was my own man, but I'd never turn down access to the family bank account. I had a career to make outside of the family business.

"We've been infiltrated!" I heard the shout coming from the stairs.

One of the doofus recruits was carrying our dog, Sanchez, under his arm. The poor thing looked as if he'd bathed in a bucket of mud—the dog, not the doofus. The three ladies I'd seen earlier canoodling with them flew down the stairs. Madison and Hailey ran after them.

From across the room, I caught sight of Preston once again performing a keg stand. His heels hit the ground hard before he ran toward the recruit, grabbing Sanchez and holding him up for all to see. The mutt didn't seem bothered at all. He lay still in Preston's hands, clinging to a bone entirely too big for his little body.

"Who did this? Who gave us a dirty Sanchez?" Preston yelled.

I stood up, ready to pounce—on Preston. I knew who had done it. The guilty party's pink hair flashed through the crowd and toward the door. We had been tricked by not only the BAD girls, but also by a Simmons. If Preston found out or caught hold of one of these girls, they'd regret ever trying to pull a prank on DIK.

One time, Preston had told me he'd purchased eighteen boxes of crickets. When the offending sorority wasn't home, the brothers let them go in the house. Not only were the sisters disgusted, but they also couldn't sleep for weeks.

And that happened right before finals. Four of the sisters failed their exams. It had been harmless but not the traditional DIK way.

"You aren't mad, are ya?" Madison shouted.

I quickly followed Madison and her sisters out the door, nodding to Preston from across the room like I had the situation under control. But he was pumped and ready to go, red-faced and sweating. He pushed the crowd out of his way, knocking over anyone who stood between him and Madison. I was already out of the door before he crossed the room. All of his beer-guzzling would slow him down. I didn't partake in a lot of drunken debaucheries. Sure, I liked a glass of whiskey now and then. But I loved my abs more.

I followed behind the girls as stealthily as I could. I didn't want to scare them, but I didn't want them to get caught by someone other than me either. I heard my brothers behind me, struggling to get out of the house. And up ahead, I heard the girls giggling, as if they didn't think this was serious. They should have known better. The worst thing you could do to an elite was laugh at them—or their dog, apparently.

I lost sight of everyone, except Hailey. She paused nearby a tree, inspecting something at its roots. I dug my heels into the ground and leaped forward, wrapping my arms around her distracting, exposed midriff and scooping her up before either of us realized what was happening. I clutched her to me as tight as she clutched the purse in her hands.

"What're you doing? Put me down!" she gasped, pummeling me with her bag.

"Calm down, damn it. I'm saving you. You don't have any idea what you're playing at."

She locked her arms around my neck and buried her head on my chest in a move I hadn't expected. I'd thought she would continue to beat me with her handbag, but instead, she cuddled me. That was when I knew that Hailey Simmons had no idea I was a Moretti.

"Why are you saving me?" She looked up. Her rosy mouth puckered dangerously close to my lips.

I had been right. She hadn't been drinking. Her breath was minty and sweet, not soaked in the dizzying scent of cheap beer.

"Because my brothers aren't going to be nice when they catch you. They've been hazing recruits all week. They're riled up for fresh meat, and you, you're as fresh as they come. They'd love to get ahold of you and your bubblegum-pink hair. Maybe I would too," I growled, imagining Preston humiliating Hailey—or worse, catching her in his arms, her body fighting against his. If Hailey didn't know who I was yet, I could give her an excellent first impression. "Such a BAD girl. I've heard stories about you ladies, but I had no idea. The dirty Sanchez prank was all sorts of wrong. But also, pretty damn funny. I'll give you that. Except … that poor dog."

"Yeah, yeah. We gave him a bone! It's not like we gave him a bad haircut. We just let him roll in the mud a bit. Like a normal dog," she huffed.

Her breasts rubbed against me with each rise and fall of her chest. My jaw tightened.

"I see. So, normal dog things. Unlike the stuff they put him through, like dressing him up in bow ties and feeding him lamb chops out of a golden bowl. What's worse than a dirty Sanchez? A pussy Sanchez. They should let him be a dog." I gripped her harder, searching for a place to hide.

The voices behind us were getting too close for my comfort.

"Didn't know a DIK would care so much about animal welfare—or my welfare actually. I can't believe you're one of them. I've never seen you before. You seem less … DIK-ish."

She swept her manicured hand along my clenched jawline until I felt the muscles in my face relax. If Hailey knew she was in the arms of a Moretti, I had no doubt she'd curl her dainty hand into a fist and beat me over the head.

The fact that she had no idea who I was only excited me even more, making me brave ... or stupid.

"Just wait." I set her down behind a tree, crushing myself into her and covering her mouth with mine before she could resist.

She sank into me as I moved my tongue over her lips, devouring her sweet gasps. I greedily lost myself in her shallow breathing. My fingers entwined in hers as I lifted her hands, pinning her delicate body against the tree. She felt so tiny and frail. I knew if I wasn't careful, I could easily break her. A Moretti breaking a Simmons—the story of our lives.

"Dominick!" Preston shouted. "Which way did they go?"

"Damn it," I whispered, tearing myself away from her. I pressed my finger to her lips and stepped out from behind the tree. "I don't know, Preston. I think they got us this time. They ran, and I couldn't keep up. We'll get them back. Let's go clean up poor Sanchez. Then, we can think straight and plot our next move." I ran off, catching Preston and turning him around before he made his way to Hailey.

If he caught her, I'd have to choose between being a DIK or saving Hailey Simmons. And despite the drama that would undoubtedly play out, I had to break my bad reputation, no matter what. I wasn't only saving her. I was saving me too.

I rolled over and grabbed my phone, bitch-buttoning whoever dared to call me at this hour. The sun wasn't even peeking through my window yet, and my phone had been vibrating nonstop beside me. I pushed the side button, declining the call three times before I was awake enough to check the name flashing across my phone.

Ma, it read.

Ma? I panicked. The way she was blowing up my phone could only mean something was wrong.

"What? What is it? You okay?" I said as soon as I answered the phone.

I threw the covers off me and hopped to my feet before stumbling back over onto the bed. My mind had woken in a panic, but my body was still half-asleep. I hadn't slept well at all, and by the looks of my sparkling clean room, I'd been sleep-walking again. I pushed myself back off the bed and moved the chair away from my bedroom door.

The last time I'd forgotten to set my chair against my door and bar myself from leaving my room in the middle of a sleepwalking trance, I'd found my way into my friend's room and peed in his drawer, mistaking it for the toilet. When I pulled my underwear down and turned around to squat, he finally stopped recording me on his phone and rushed to stop me, waking me into a disorientated and humiliated state. It had taken a lot of convincing and even bribery to get him to hand over the video and not make it viral.

Friend. Right.

I'd isolated myself after that incident. That had been two years ago, and I'd become mostly a lone wolf since then, much to my family's dissatisfaction. My father wanted me to network and make connections. I was a Moretti, he'd said. I needed to be seen and heard and command the room, blah, blah, blah. He pushed me to become one of those obnoxious people who talked loud enough for everyone to notice them, hence my membership to the DIK fraternity.

At this new school, I had a fresh start, and the first thing I had done was make sure a chair sat wedged against my bedroom door. I wouldn't piss on anyone in the DIK house. Not unintentionally anyway. Truth be told, my fraternity brothers weren't entirely asshats. We had a few good seeds and a few bad apples. Thus was life.

Preston had taken me under his wing, and although he could be a bit much to handle most days, he seemed to have a warm heart hidden in there somewhere. I glimpsed pieces of it now and then.

"What're you thinking, son? A Simmons? Really? You could have any woman you wanted! But, no, you decide on having the one you can't!" my mom barked into the phone.

"What? How did you—" I started. A wave of heat flushed through me, settling into my chest.

"Because apparently, you ran across Father Baker's lawn with a pink-haired princess in your arms. I don't think there's a lot of pink-haired princesses at FU. I only know of one."

"How do you know Hailey Simmons has pink hair?" I gulped, sitting back on my bed and pulling the covers up over me.

"I follow all the local social magazines! How do you not?"

"Ugh, I guess I don't follow all of the social magazines."

"Don't get smart with me. Hailey and that Sheffield girl are all over the place. They're one of those social sensations. Or pariahs. Or whatever it's called. They have their hands in everything and anything, and they have a huge following. You're lucky Father Baker called me and not your dad. You can't hide with a pink-haired princess who shares the same last name as our enemy, so don't try it."

I pinched the bridge of my nose, trying to take in everything she'd said.

"So, Hailey is a socialite. That's not so bad. It could be worse. Father Baker could have ratted my ass out, saying I was carrying a meth head through his front lawn."

"Dominick Nicholi Moretti! You know how serious this is."

"Oh, right. They don't do meth at FU. It's coke and Adderall. I forgot that meth is for community colleges."

"I'm going to call the driver to get you and show you how funny this is if you don't listen up. Your father can't find out about this, Dom. Find yourself a normal girl. Someone low-key, smart, bright, fun, classy. Someone you can carry wherever you want, and it won't be written about in the local papers or blogs or whatever the hell they use these days."

"Are you saying I'm forbidden to hang out with her because she's a Simmons? What exactly happened between our fathers? Why can't I even mention their name without Dad's face boiling red? I didn't do anything. Hailey didn't do anything. So, why are we being punished?"

"Oh, Dom. I'm not going back down that road. Just trust me. I don't want to see you hurt. I'm sure she's getting the same speech right now if her parents know she was with you."

"I don't think she knew who I was, Ma. It's not like you're thinking. She was at the party, and her sorority played a prank on the fraternity. I wanted to save Hailey before my brothers got to her. Don't worry. DIK didn't see me being chivalrous. My bad reputation is still on the line." I huffed a breath out of my nose for emphasis but only managed a squeaking booger whistle. I sounded like a drowning mouse and felt like one too. When I dealt with my dad, I only became stronger. But my ma could reduce me to a helpless bug under her alligator-hide shoe.

"Saving the girl. As much as I admire honor in you, you also need to know there are boundaries in life. We can't always get what we want. Even for a Moretti, there are things you can't have. She's one of them." She sighed.

I heard the clinking of a spoon and mug in the background and knew she was sitting in the sunroom, curled into an armchair, waiting for the sun to rise.

For years, I'd sat out there with her until I outgrew our ritual and preferred sleep over dawn. Sometimes, when I came home for holidays, I'd sneak out there to spend time with her again. I could tell by the way her face lit up that she missed those moments. I was her only son, and with my dad traveling and building hotels internationally now, she led a lonely life and often seemed sad.

"But—" I began.

"But! You know I hate that word. No buts. Your father and I let you come back and do this damn vet school you'd begged to attend. We got you in there, and we got you in the top fraternity at FU. You've gotten enough wants. Leave the girl alone. *La famiglia prima di tutto.* Family first," she snapped before taking a loud sip of her coffee.

"I know; I know. Family comes first. I'll keep my distance," I said, gritting my teeth and putting the thought of Hailey out of my mind.

I didn't have a chance with her anyway. People were reporting my personal business around town, and Hailey would find out who I was soon enough. And after whatever my parents had done to hers, she wouldn't want anything to do with me. I couldn't blame her. I'd steer clear of a Moretti too.

"Thank you. Now, go back to sleep. Get your rest and save some animals tomorrow. Animals. Not Simmons girls."

"Wait. There are more Simmons girls?"

"No! That's not what I meant. She's the one and only. I thought you were dropping this?"

"It's dropped. It's dropped!" I said more to myself than her.

I had a feeling I'd have to continually remind myself to stop thinking about Hailey over the next few days until she was clearly out of my head.

"Good. I'll see you for Sunday dinner. I love you."

I felt the tension through the phone evaporate into thin air. Whatever drama I'd caused for my mom must have worried her enough to let her poker face slip.

"Love you too." I hung up the phone.

I lay my head back on the pillow, too frazzled to go back to sleep. The only thing I could think of was the way Hailey had felt in my arms. The sweet way she'd rested her head against me felt anything but wrong. I knew I was supposed to forget about her, but one last thought wouldn't hurt anyone.

I slipped my underwear down over my knees and took my cock in my hand. It had already grown hard at the first thought of Hailey's pouty mouth, slightly parted. Her breasts had jostled against my chest with each step I took while we made our escape last night. I hadn't planned on kissing her. I'd only planned on helping her get away. But the way Hailey's eyes became hooded when she caressed my jaw gave me the green light. I'd pinned her up against the tree a lot gentler than I wanted.

If I could have my way with Hailey Simmons, I'd fuck us both into a rough penance, paying for whatever sins we bore from our families so we could start anew. She wouldn't be a Simmons, and I wouldn't be a Moretti. We could just be Hailey and me. Free to do whatever the fuck we wanted, like each other.

I stroked my cock and imagined how she would feel, wrapped around me. And in a euphoric daze, thinking with the wrong head, I decided to fix this dumb situation I had been forced into and save the girl.

Three

HAILEY

I sketched matching damask-print lingerie in my notebook, oblivious to whatever my Industry Communications professor kept droning on and on about. She paced the front of the room, clicking through slide after slide of pure boredom. I rubbed my eyes and rested my head on my hand, slouching down in my seat. Industry Communications was one of those dreaded course requirements everyone hated.

Sitting in a room, learning about outdated or even archaic styling advice, was my least favorite part of college. I preferred to spend my time in the fashion studio—sewing, designing, and working on projects with my hands. I wasn't into studying books or leading presentations. My creativity thrived with pins, a tape measure, and old-school renderings on paper—not the designing software we used these days. I was up-to-date on the latest and greatest tech, but I hated it. Keeping up with social media and computer programs took time away from what I really loved—creating.

"And with that, we're done for today. See you next week," the professor said to a class full of students already scrambling out of their seats.

I grabbed my bag and headed toward Joel's apartment complex across campus. I'd texted him last night that I wanted to meet for lunch. He couldn't be bothered with actually taking me out, so instead, he invited me over to his place. I didn't care this time. I only had one thing on my mind, and it wasn't the inevitable breakup looming over my head. What I needed now was to get laid.

I hadn't had sex with my boyfriend in over six weeks. I'd hinted around several times that I was primed and ready, but he rarely took the bait. I'd poke my butt out and up against him when we lay on the couch, watching movies, or I'd put my hand on his thigh, lingering a bit too long while he played his games. I'd bat my lashes and lean my cleavage in his face, but he'd swat me away. I'd even taken a striptease exercise class and tried to give him a lap dance once. I'd fallen on my ass, and he'd just rolled his eyes.

I had done everything I knew how to do to get him to notice me, but it never worked. He never noticed me. Joel was too busy wrapped up in his friends and games. I was left dry, he was left high, and my avoidant personality let him get away with it. I knew I needed to end it. I planned on giving him the boot soon enough. But today, I couldn't think about drama. Today, all I could think about was my lickable enemy, Dominick.

The only thing on my mind lately had been the damn passionate encounter with him at the frat party. But I couldn't exactly go romping around with a man as dangerous as a Moretti. So, I played it safe and decided to romp around with my boyfriend and just pretend it was Dominick. I would swap their faces while I rode to O-town and be good to go. I was excellent at acting, and besides, I had a bag of tricks with me this time. Literally.

I carried a super-sexy anime girl's outfit, wrapped at the bottom of my purse, along with my trusty vibe. I knew Joel liked that cartoon type of stuff, and after some digging into the kink, I stumbled upon Ahegao porn. I'd never heard of it myself. But the fake cartoonish vibe seemed like something that might turn my man on, and I'd do anything to feel desired again. I doubted he could ravish me up against a tree as Dominick had, but I would sure as hell entice him to try.

I'd stayed up for an extra hour last night, practicing my Ahegao expressions in the mirror and drawing my makeup on so I looked like a woman on his screen—big-eyed and slack-mouthed. If this fantasy didn't do the trick for him, he was as hopeless as I'd thought. Still, I had to try to set aside my basic-bitch tendencies and do something out of my comfort zone even if this act required a little more confidence than I pretended to have.

I stuck my chin out and clacked my heels on the cobblestone path leading to his apartment. Joel's parents, like most parents at FU, funded his living expenses. He could have pledged to a fraternity or rented a house on Greek Row. But instead, he'd chosen to live nearby his friends in this shady apartment complex. No doubt, he'd rather live a life of convenience rather than reign supreme. His lack of motivation was extremely unattractive, and yet here I was.

"Looking good, Hailey! Yow!" Steve, one of Joel's dopey friends, called from a balcony above me. A cloud of smoke billowed out in front of him as he vaped his douche nozzle.

I held my breath and scrunched my nose at the sickeningly sweet, artificial watermelon scent wafting down. I didn't want to breathe that shit. There was no telling what it could do to brain cells. By the looks of Steve and the rest of Joel's friends, whatever they smoked or drank worked like a brain-eating amoeba, devouring what little intelligence they had and leaving them a sad lump of dumbass. I picked up my pace until I reached Joel's door, knocking loud enough for him to hear me over his game.

"Hey there. Come in. I'm in a match. Give me one sec." Joel answered the door without even looking at me. He left it open before adjusting his headset and running back to his computer.

"Ah, gaming. Figures," I muttered, shutting the door and sighing.

I had no idea if or when he went to class. School rarely came up in our short conversations. He didn't ask me about the sorority or fashion academy, and I didn't question his lack of effort for his future. Aside from our love of Thai food, we didn't have much in common, except wealthy parents.

"I'm going to use your bathroom real quick," I said to the back of his head.

I stepped over a pile of dirty laundry and into a decently clean bathroom. Joel's parents sent him their cleaning person twice a week. Otherwise, I wouldn't set foot in his place. He had a nasty habit of leaving old food lying around, missing the toilet, and clogging the sink with his scraggly chin pubes.

I rifled through my bag, which was similar to a magical Mary Poppins satchel. I could fit anything and everything in this bad bitch. Just today, I'd stuffed my lingerie, books, notebooks, pens, folders, condoms—because my lame boyfriend was too lazy to buy them—a hair straightener, and my new vibe—because, again, my boyfriend was lazy—inside of it and still had room to spare.

I unwrapped my anime-girl costume and cursed myself for not trying it on earlier. This wasn't what I'd ordered at all, but I slipped into it anyway. The cheap material scratched against my skin. I'd ordered a small, but this outfit felt child-sized. The bad stitching throughout clung to my body, giving me rolls, like a busted can of biscuits. I stood in front of the mirror and tugged at the strings of what was basically a faux metal bikini. I looked like a Roman warrior, not some Japanese princess. I shrugged my shoulders, busting a seam.

Oh well, it will be off in a few minutes anyway.

I sauntered out of the bathroom and over to Joel, standing in front of him. I mentally counted to ten before he looked up to see the Ahegao expression I'd practiced. I stuck my tongue out, rolling it to the side while crossing my eyes and moaning. I grabbed my breasts, tugging my costume down and making a high-pitched moan.

"Um, what the fuck is this? Are you trying to make me get off my game?" He pulled off his headphones and set them aside.

I snapped my eyes to his and flinched. "It's an anime costume, and I'm doing the Ahegao shit you're into. You know, where the cartoon girls make *come fuck me* faces? Like this!" I opened my mouth wide and stuck my tongue out again, making another face. "I thought you'd like it, considering you can't tear your eyes away from them on your screen. Not even to look at your half-naked girlfriend, practically begging to be touched, right in front of you!"

"You look like you're having a stroke. I've never seen anime girls make a face like that! Besides, I think you're wearing a superhero costume or something. What were you thinking?" He threw his head back and laughed, clutching his sides. "Are you a gladiator? Fuck, this is gold. Hold on. Let me snap a pic."

He reached for his phone, but I'd already fled back to the bathroom. I sniffled back a sob, wiping the tears off my face with the back of my hand.

Gladiator. What the fuck? I will fucking this is Sparta his ass out of that damn gaming chair and clear across the room if he comes near me again. Bastard!

"Open up. I'm sorry, Hailey. I didn't mean it like that." Joel knocked on the door, still muffling his laughter.

I flung it open and barreled past him. He smelled like an overcooked egg anyway and didn't look much better.

"I'm pretty sure the laugh you gave me for trying was real. We're done. It's through. I'm out. I don't even know why I've stayed this long," I spit out, marching through his front door.

"Wait! I said, I'm sorry. Hold on! You can't walk out of here like that! You're half-naked!" He ran after me, following on my heels.

"Oh, now, you notice when I'm naked!" I lowered my head and walked faster.

"Hailey?" a voice called from down the path.

I looked up just in time to see Dominick walking toward me with Sanchez on a leash.

"Hailey. Stop!" Joel reached out, grabbing my arm and jerking me around.

I lost my footing and stumbled.

"Whoa. Whoa. Whoa. Don't grab her like that!" Dominick ran to my side, towering over Joel.

Sanchez growled the non-scariest growl I'd ever heard. It was cuter and cuddlier than it was threatening.

"Who the hell are you? This is my girlfriend. She's fine. Aren't you?" Joel tugged at my arm.

I snatched it back and sneered, "I'm not yours. I'm not pixelated enough." I held my bag in front of me, blocking Joel from coming closer and shielding my half-naked body from both of them.

"You don't know what you're talking about. You—" Joel started, reaching out again.

Dominick dropped Sanchez's leash and stepped between us. "I think she knows exactly what she means, and you do too. Don't touch her again," Dominick said through clenched teeth. His eyes shot back and forth, scanning Joel's face.

I watched as the legendary Italian temper simmered just below his surface.

I couldn't see Joel from over Dominick's massive shoulders, but I was sure he only shrugged before leaving. I wasn't worth fighting for—to him at least.

Dominick turned back toward me once Joel disappeared.

"Never thought I'd run into Red Sonja today. Or Pink Sonja. I don't know what your story is, but I'd love for you to whisper it in my ear." He grinned before picking up Sanchez's leash. The dog had remained where Dominick left him.

"Who's Pink Sonja?" I sniffled, taking a step back.

"Your costume. Don't you know who you're dressed up as? She's a comic book hero from the '70s and '80s. She's a badass. You know *Conan*? She started there." Dominick spoke to my eyes and not my half-naked body. Though I could tell by the way he tipped his chin back that he was fighting the urge to take a long look at my jiggly bits.

"Who's Conan?" I asked.

He slapped his forehead and groaned. "You don't know who Conan the Barbarian is either? Wow!"

"No. I'm sorry I don't keep up with all this men's fantasy stuff. I'm too busy to get caught up in cartoons!" I pulled my purse closer to me, clutching it for warmth. I heard a click before my entire bag began to vibrate. That was the only downside to my new vibe. It could get me off in two minutes flat, but the rumbling noise it made sounded like a rocket engine preparing to blast me off. And it did. Easily. So easily.

"Um, I think you're buzzing." He jerked his thumb toward my bag.

My face flushed a shade of red that clashed with my pink hair, doing me no favors. I'd already looked like a hot mess.

"I don't know what you're talking about." I pushed the purse into my chest, two, four, eight times, desperately trying to turn my vibrator back off.

"Sure you do. It's that loud-ass vibrator you're carrying around with you or some kind of ticking time bomb," he said. "Sexy cosplay costume and a vibrator. I'd say the douche bag had it good today. And by the looks of the mascara running down your face, I'd also say he royally fucked it up. What a shame." He clicked his tongue.

I buried my blushing face in my bag, digging around until I found my vibrator and switched it off. I kept my head down, fiddling around, avoiding his gaze. I didn't know how to save this situation. I hoped he would get bored and just walk away eventually. But I knew a Moretti wasn't one to give up. A cool breeze blew by, sending a waft of stale watermelon fumes down on me from where Joel's friend sat, watching our every move.

Dominick looked up and quickly back down again.

"Follow me." He motioned toward an alcove and tugged on Sanchez's leash.

I nodded, following behind him.

"Take this." He stretched, peeling off his jacket and draping it over me.

I shifted my eyes away from his form-fitting tee, wrapped snug across his broad chest. His nipples peeked through, erect and lickable. His thick forearms were decorated with a wide range of tattoos, entirely out of character for a frat boy. I couldn't imagine Dominick dressed in khakis and polo shirts with wraparound glasses hanging off the tip of his perfect nose. I wondered what someone who looked like him was doing in such a stuffy frat house anyway.

"I can't wear your jacket. I'll be fine," I lied, shimmying out of his jacket and handing it back. My skin prickled. I wasn't fine. I was humiliated, recently broken up, freezing my boobs off, and standing in an alcove with my worst enemy who looked like he should be off modeling underwear or dazzling the paparazzi—not walking a lapdog and staring hungrily at me.

"Why? Because you can't take anything from a Moretti?"

"No. I mean, yes. I mean"—I jutted my hip out—"maybe. You know I can't be seen with you. Or your jacket. If my family found out—"

"Mine already did. My priest saw me carrying you across his lawn at the frat party. He rang my mom, and she rang me the next morning. It looks like we both have eyes watching out for us—or watching us anyway. I wouldn't say my parents know what's best for me, but they like to think they do. I'm not like them, you know. I'm not like my dad." He slung the jacket over his shoulder like an '80s high school heartthrob.

"You go to church?" I blinked, leaning in to make sure I'd heard him right.

"Is that all you got out of our convo?"

"It was a distracting tidbit of information."

"I used to go. Italian, Catholic. Goes hand in hand. At least, my family is serious about it. I kind of do my own thing now." He shrugged.

"So, you don't go to church?" I asked.

"Is this a trick question? Are you judging me?"

"Forget it! Just turn around and cover me." I gave a dismissive wave of my hand.

"You're going to get naked? Here? In the middle of the apartment complex? You can't do that! Just take this."

He held his jacket out to me again, but I pushed it away.

"Are you telling me what I can and can't do? Typical." My nostrils flared.

"Ugh. There's no winning with you, is there?" He shook his head at me before putting his jacket back on in overemphasized movements.

"Nope. Not when your last name starts with an *M*, ends with an *I*, and rhymes with spaghetti," I said, sighing as he covered his bangable body back up.

"Manchetti?" He raised his brows.

"Wrong."

"Mumbetti!"

"Yeah, no."

"Maletti."

"Keep it up, and I'll stick you with a machete!" I laughed.

"That's morbid! Besides, I'm looking at you now, and there's no place for you to hide a machete in the tiny little costume you're wearing. I couldn't even find a spot to hide my pocketknife." His gaze raked over my body, pausing at my breasts.

"Look at this bag!" I held it up, blocking his view. "Don't you know I could fit a camel in here if I wanted to?" My teeth chattered.

"A camel, huh? Look, you're cold. And stubborn. I get it. I'm the Devil's spawn. Rawr. But let me help you. To make up for the kiss I threw at you the other night. That wasn't very gentlemanlike. I didn't know you had a boyfriend either, or I wouldn't have done it."

"You didn't ask."

"Do you have a boyfriend?" he asked, stepping into me.

The scent of whatever cologne he wore made my head spin and my legs spread.

"Not anymore," I answered, taking a step back into the brick wall.

He had me cornered. Again.

"So, are you telling me, I'm free to kiss you?" The corner of his mouth turned up into a smirk.

"I didn't say that! I said—"

He pushed me against the wall, covering my body with his and pressing his lips against mine before I had a chance to explain myself. His palm slid up my thigh, caressing my goose-bumped flesh before pulling the string on my bikini bottom in one swift motion. I gasped. The bottom half of my costume hung down, barely covering my vag.

"I think I found that camel toe you were hiding," he whispered into my mouth before pushing himself off of me. He whirled around, stretching out his jacket and shielding me from anyone who might walk our way.

"It was a camel! Not a camel toe." I blew out a breath while stepping out of my costume and into my clothes. "You'd better keep your eyes forward, Moretti. And now, you owe me twice. You can't just kiss me like you own me." My voice shook.

The sexual tension I'd built up since our last encounter was still there and growing. But I couldn't do anything about it. Not with him anyway. He was forbidden, like Pandora's box or Eve's apple. One bite of Dominick, and life as I knew it would be over.

"I saved you from my frat brothers, your boyfriend, and possibly going viral once you walked across campus, dressed like that. I think it's the other way around. You owe me."

"I can save myself, thanks!" I stuffed my costume back into my bag and stepped beside him.

"Can you?" He turned toward me.

"Well, maybe not all the time. But I can make you believe it."

"You can try." He brushed the pad of his thumb over my bottom lip before turning to leave. "Convince me at Bar Thomas. Friday at seven! It's '80s night. The perfect time to wear a disguise," he called over his shoulder.

"What if I already have plans on Friday?" I shouted back.

"What if?" His lips spread into an enticing smile, dazzling me into canceling whatever plans I had for the next two years.

I took a deep breath and rubbed the tension building in my shoulders. I had to tell Madison. Dominick was right. I couldn't save myself, not when he was around.

I'd been sitting, curled in a leather chair, thumbing through *Vogue*'s latest issues while waiting for Madison. The common room was the central hub for my sorority sisters. But tonight, the room was dead, and I had the place to myself. Wednesdays were reserved for girls' night out.

I stacked my fashion magazines next to a candle, put a cup of tea on top of them, and hashtagged studying before posting the picture to my social media. In a matter of minutes, my phone buzzed with notifications. So-and-so liked my photo, another person commented, one person tagged me, and eighteen people gave me hearts. I scrolled through my news feed, landing on a picture of Joel with his arm around a girl who looked vaguely familiar. He stood, laughing, throwing his hand up in a peace sign. She stuck her tongue out in that half-lidded way he'd laughed at me for doing. I zoomed in on the picture.

A friend of Joel's had posted it ten minutes ago and checked into their location as Joel's crib. Sure enough, I noticed the gaming desk in the background against the drab hospital-beige walls.

"That asshole," I muttered.

It hadn't been but a few hours, and Joel already had another woman, which meant he'd probably had her all along. I clenched my jaw and kept scrolling, desperate to get my mind off of my douche-bag ex, who didn't deserve to spend any time in my thoughts. Before I knew what I was doing, I typed *Delta Iota Kappa* in the search bar and brought up the fraternity's social media pages, clicking until I found Dominick.

I scrolled through photos until I landed on one of him with his arms around the same girl in the photo with Joel. Her tongue was stuck out sideways in this picture too.

What the hell?

I checked the time on the post. It was from three months ago. Only Dominick was tagged in the photo. I clicked his name and crossed my fingers that his profile was public. The page loaded, full of pictures with him, Preston, and other fraternity members I'd met once or twice before. I kept scrolling until a picture of Dominick and this girl popped up again. They were dressed as if attending a gala. I didn't want to admit it, but she cleaned up nicely. Her hair was tied back in a French twist, and her thin arms were draped over Dominick's broad shoulders. I stiffened.

Of course, with my luck, there wasn't a name tagged to the picture. I took a sip of my tea and tried to zoom in on the photo to measure myself up against this woman who was making her rounds with my men.

"What're you doing? You look like an old lady, curled in a blanket in the corner! At least, I hope it's cashmere." Madison glided on her trendy flats across the floor and over to me.

I tried to close the picture, but my thumb slipped and instead pushed the little heart icon next to his photo.

"Shit!" I panicked. "Oh no. Oh no. Oh no."

"What's going on?" Madison plopped herself in the leather chair beside me and stretched out her legs. She held her feet up and turned them side to side, admiring her shoes.

"I need your help!" I cried.

"Good. I need yours too," she replied.

"This is an emergency!" I set my phone down and stood up, pacing the floor.

"Me too!" she said, throwing her hands in the air. "Most of the recruits are great, but we can't take them all in. There are these two girls who—"

"Madison!" I stopped in front of her. "I kissed Dominick Moretti, and I just stalked his profile and accidentally liked one of his pictures of him and some woman." I wrinkled my nose at the thought of her.

"You kissed Dominick Moretti?" Her eyes grew wide, and she made the perfect slack-jawed expression I'd failed to make.

"Yes. And now, he wants to meet me for a date at Bar Thomas on Friday."

"Hold up. You're dating the son of your family's archenemy, and you didn't tell me? Your BFF? I'm appalled!" She slapped her cheeks and gasped.

I'd never seen someone as dramatic as Madison. Once, when another sorority sister had suggested we cut our expenses for a month and repurpose old clothes, Madison had slumped in her seat, falling off her chair and rolling to the other side of the common room. That had been the end of the conversation.

"I'll explain. But first, what do I do? Do I unlike his picture? If I do it, he'll still see it in his notifications and know I didn't do it on purpose. He'll know I was stalking! But if I leave it, he'll still know I was stalking! Help!"

A group of girls walked through the door and up the stairs. Cheri trailed behind with an armload of shopping bags.

"Are you two okay? You look like someone died." Cheri paused before heading up to her room.

I cut my eyes to Madison and mouthed for her to zip it.

"Yep. Just discussing the recruits. What's in the bags?" Madison expertly diverted the conversation.

"Oh, you know, just a few things"—Cheri craned her neck around to make sure the other girls were gone—"for work." She winked before running up the stairs.

"Continue." Madison narrowed her eyes. "And let me see your phone."

I tossed my phone in her lap. "Help. He's going to think I'm a stalker!"

"That's not your biggest problem. Your biggest problem is, you're fucking a Moretti."

"I'm not fucking him! It was a kiss. Two. It just happened." I sat back down on the chair, pulling my legs up under me and hugging them.

A notification dinged from my phone.

"*Well, well, well. Look who decided to play super sleuth and do some digging. If you want to appear incognito on Friday, you'll need to be sneakier and wear a disguise. I wouldn't be opposed to you wearing your Red Sonja outfit again,*" Madison read aloud. "What does that mean?"

"Give me that." I grabbed the phone from her hand. "I tried some stupid lingerie move with Joel, and he shut me down. I broke up with him and ran out of his apartment and into Dominick. He helped me get away from Joel and covered my ass while I dressed. Then, he kissed me. He'd also kissed me on the night of the frat party. When you ran off and left me behind, he scooped me up and helped me get away." I stared at his text on my phone.

"You broke up with Joel? I'm so proud of you!" She jumped out of her seat and clapped before sitting back down. "But this Moretti mistake can't happen again. I hope you don't plan on meeting him."

"I was going to ask to borrow one of your wigs," I said. "Shit."

"Look, I'll be careful, but you can't mention this again. It's a one-time thing. Maybe he'll apologize for his family, and the drama will be put to rest. Then, all will be well in the world!" I threw my hands in the air and swallowed my bullshit.

"If you two get caught, do you have any idea how fast your parents or his will find out? You'll be cut from your trust fund. Then what? You'll be kicked out of the academy, the sorority, even Forks maybe! You'll die lonely, wearing last season's trends. You're playing with fire. You know it. I know it. That damn Moretti knows it. It could be a trap, and you're walking straight into it. He's a DIK. He's probably getting us back for our dirty Sanchez! I bet he's working with Preston," she spit out those last words.

I leaned my head back on the chair and thought about how to respond to Madison and Dominick.

"I'll be on guard. Just let me borrow a wig. I'll squash it. But, Madison?"

She shook her head and sighed. "What?"

"Don't ever tell anyone. Please? Ride or die. Snitches get stitches."

"Don't I know it? I've cross-stitched plenty into my shit list. If it's what you want, I'll help. But I don't want anything to do with Preston or the rest of DIK. I'm helping my sister out, not anyone from his side."

"Thanks. No one will know. It's just me and you and him. If someone finds out, it's on him. But I don't think he's the type to snitch. He seems ... not how I'd expect a Moretti."

"Careful. That's what they're known for, ya know. That and their mob ties. Snakes in the grass. Turn your head for a split second, and they'll crush you before swallowing you whole. Ask your dad." She inspected her nails. The tips had been filed off to points that looked painfully dangerous.

"Maybe I will. I've never understood the drama between our families anyway."

"Fine. Don't say—"

"You warned me. I know," I said, pinching the bridge of my nose to ward off a stress headache. I shook my head and texted back a short response to Dominick.

Me: Doing my due diligence, so I don't end up with cement boots. They'd clash with the costume.

Dominick: Don't worry. I won't tell if you won't. Snitches get stitches.

I smiled into my phone until Madison interrupted my dreamy trance with her squawking.

She smacked a rolled-up magazine against the table. "Damn it, Hailey! You're already getting goofy-eyed over there. Don't lose focus and forget rule number one: besties before testes. We're here to be boss babes. Now, help me with this recruit situation. I need ideas on how to handle this year's candidates."

"Okay, okay." I set my phone aside. "But first, should I go as fierce redhead Jessica Rabbit or bottled-blonde Madonna? I called the costume shop, and that's all they had left."

"Ugh," Madison groaned. "Red. Like a warning label. Now, pose." She held her phone up, pursed her lips, and snapped a selfie of the both of us. She posted it to her public profile and tagged me. The hashtag read *double trouble.*

With friends like Madison, I didn't need a warning label.

DOMINICK

The streets in front of Bar Thomas were jammed with cars. The new restaurant had recently opened its doors for the first time, and the fancy liberal arts majors had quickly declared the bar the new place to be seen. But I didn't socialize much with the liberal arts crowd. I stuck with the elites, who ventured closer to downtown on weekends. I'd picked the perfect, cozy spot to mingle with Hailey. The lively band would surely drown our private conversations, and the dark corners would hide us from prying eyes. Not that I expected anyone to notice us in costume.

I pushed my way inside and passed the expansive wooden bar. The mixologists behind the counter tossed around bottles, shook shakers, and flambéed the tops of their crafty cocktails to the oohs and aahs of the young crowd. People stood elbow to elbow, dressed in wind suits, leotards, and bad hairdos. I even passed by a man with a huge, hairy dildo strapped on his face, only to realize later that he was dressed as ALF.

I slid into a booth in the back, wiping hardened crumbs off the seat. The band began to play oldies tunes I hadn't heard in years. The songs brought me back to the weekends I'd spent traveling with my parents to and from events I hated. It was always *see and be seen* with my parents, and I preferred the humble life of not showing off whatever new toy our sketchy income had bought.

"Yo, Bowie. Can I get you anything?" a waitress asked, stopping by my table. She wore plastic hoop earrings the size of my fist and fuchsia lipstick that caked at the corners of her lips. A shimmery blue stripe highlighted a bead of sweat just under her arched brows.

"I'll take whatever IPA you have on tap. Thanks," I said, brushing my blond wig out of my face.

I pulled up my ruffled sleeve and checked the time on my watch. I was old school and still chose to wear a real watch and not one of those smartwatches that kept reminding me to breathe or slow my heart rate down. I didn't want anyone barking orders at me. Besides, I didn't trust technology. I posted on social media here and there to appease my parents and friends. Otherwise, I would love to live off-grid and out of the public eye. But everyone knew a Moretti, just like everyone knew a Simmons. And those two together were dangerous.

The waitress set my beer on the table before hobbling off in her neon-thonged Jazzercise leotard. I settled into my booth, watching the door like a hawk. I wondered if Hailey would take my disguise request seriously. She had just as much to lose as I did. The room filled with groups of students, dressed in head to toe '80s gear. There was a handful of Madonnas, rock stars, Goonies, and a whole lot of neon and spandex.

I took a long gulp of my beer right as Jessica Rabbit walked through the entrance. My jaw dropped, my eyes bulged, and I wanted to yell, *Aooga! Aooga!* But that could draw attention to us, and J. Rab and I didn't want that. I immediately knew this 'toon was Hailey. The way she gripped her clutch in her gloved fist was the same way she had hung on to her bag for dear life when I carried her away from my brothers. There was no mistaking her pose.

Hailey scanned the room before spotting me and my goofy grin. She put one heel in front of the other and swung her hips side to side. She flipped her long red hair back behind her and flashed me her exposed shoulders and extra-bouncy cleavage. I touched my chin, making sure my head wasn't bobbling in sync with each jiggle of her breasts.

"You remind me of a super-sexy babe," I said, motioning for her to sit.

"I'm the super-sexy babe with the power." She smirked, smoothing down her sequined dress before sitting across from me.

"I don't doubt it. How did you know it was me anyway?" I patted my mullet wig.

"Your smile. You have a very flashy grin." She wiggled her way to the corner of the booth. Her eyes darted back and forth, surveying the room.

"Relax. No one's going to know it's you," I said.

"You did."

"Only because you carry your handbag like someone's going to snatch it from you."

"Hmmph." She set her clutch down on the table and folded her arms over her barely covered chest. One wrong move and she'd have a much-welcomed wardrobe malfunction.

"Eyes up here, Moretti." Her voice fell flat. "I mean, Goblin King."

"Eh, sorry. I'm usually much more of a gentleman. But Jessica Rabbit has always been a fantasy of mine."

"Ugh. What's with you men and cartoons?" She sighed, brushing a loose sequin off her collar.

"Well, we're men. Most of us never grow up."

"You can say that again."

"I didn't say all of us. Some of us can still be men, Hailey." Her name rolled off my tongue as smooth as the moves I planned to put on her.

"Not all men. I get it." She looked back toward the exit.

"You're scared, aren't you? Worried someone will see us? We're in the dark corner of a booth, where none of our crowd goes, dressed in costumes, and you think someone will notice us?"

"How do you know what my crowd is?"

Her eyebrows pinched together, and I knew Preston was right. These BAD girls were going to be tough nuts to crack.

"Only because I know our crowds are the same. It's been that way since childhood. The only reason why we aren't best friends is because our parents hate each other. Otherwise, you and I would have probably fucked by now." I leaned forward, resting my elbows on the table, and immediately regretted what I'd said.

"You're such a Moretti. You can't just talk to me like that," she snarled, leaning forward too.

She stretched across the table, inches from my face. I wasn't sure if I was about to get kissed or head-butted.

"That came out entirely wrong. I didn't mean it in a douche-bag way. I meant it because, when I touch your skin, I get tingles under my fingertips. And when I kissed you, I felt you hold your breath until I let you go."

I reached for her hand and twirled my index finger over her palm. She snatched her hand away and leaned back in the booth.

"Maybe you felt tingles. But I felt nothing." She cleared her throat and looked away before busying herself with the cocktail menu.

"Hmm. Keep telling yourself that." I finished my beer. "I'm going to grab another drink. What can I get you? What loosens you up? We're here to have fun. The band's playing, and we're in disguise. Let's make the most of the night even if you do hate my guts. Despite my saving you twice now."

"I don't hate your guts," she said. "Just get me an On the Rox cocktail. The one with the Shizzle Sauce, please. Thanks."

"Right. I mean, fo' shizzle." I pushed myself out of the booth and stood up, stretching my arms over my head.

"What. Is. That?" She put her gloved hand to her mouth and stifled a laugh. Tears welled in the corners of her eyes.

"What? This?" I shook my bulge around. I'd stuffed my tight leggings with not one, but three socks before leaving the frat house. I'd snuck out the back door and hopped into my Jeep before any brothers noticed and gave me a hard time.

"Duh. It's the bulge. It's basically the star of *Labyrinth*, which just so happens to be the best movie ever! Do you like it? My fake dong, not the movie … or both actually," I mused.

Hailey reached for a napkin and dabbed her eyes.

"I think you need to magic dance to the men's room and readjust. Your dark crystals are falling down your leg."

I looked down at my crotch and noticed one of my socks bulging mid-thigh. "Fuck!"

I hobbled off to the men's room, covering my bits with my hands. Her laughter roared above the band.

After I successfully readjusted my fake balls, I elbowed my way to the front of the bar and ordered the princess her drink. I looked back at our booth and caught sight of her holding her phone at an angle, pushing out her bottom lip and snapping selfie after selfie. She turned her head this way and that, arching one brow and then two. I walked back over to her, catching her gaze. She narrowed her eyes at me and hastily put her phone down. The blush creeping into her cheeks was as red as her ballgown.

"Mind if I sit beside you, so I can watch the band, Little Miss Socialite?" I scooted next to her, placing the cocktail on the table.

"Relax. I didn't post it——yet. I don't use social media because I love it. I do it because I have to keep up appearances. It's one of our sorority rules."

She stirred the straw in her glass before taking a tiny sip and licking her lips. The sight of her tongue gave my real balls a twitch.

"You guys have rules?" I asked.

"You don't?"

"Nope. Pretty much anything goes in DIK." I tilted my head back and forth, thinking about how to rephrase what I'd just said. The mental image caused me to shudder.

"Figures," she muttered.

"What's that supposed to mean?" I said to her collar. I couldn't help it. The little nook between her neck and shoulder was begging for me to nibble it. I tried to tear my eyes away, but the tiny pulse thumping under her skin had me in a trance.

"It just means you're a DIK. And a Moretti. That's two strikes." She took another sip of her drink. Her foot bobbed up and down under the table, knocking against me.

"Can I make it three?" I asked, sidling my hip next to hers.

The band started up their rendition of "Tainted Love," drowning out my voice. The urge to feel her skin on my lips kept growing, causing my manners to fly out the window.

"What? I can't hear you," she yelled into my ear. Her breath tickled my cheek.

I curled my fist, trying to restrain myself from touching her.

"I asked if I could make it three," I yelled back.

"Three what?" Her chest rose and fell faster and faster.

She could pretend she didn't want it just as bad as I wanted it. But in my blood, I was still a Moretti, and we weren't easily conned.

I leaned in and pressed my lips to the bare skin on her shoulder. She tasted like I'd imagined—just as buttery and soft as frosting on a cupcake.

"Can I get you two anything to eat? Sorry, I've been so busy, going back and forth with these younger kids tonight! They drink like fish." The waitress stopped at our table, interrupting me before I could bite.

I looked to Hailey, who only shook her head. Her hand brushed against the spot I'd just kissed.

"We're good. Thanks." I flashed the waitress a dismissive smile and hoped she got the hint to take a hike for a while. "As I was saying," I continued, whispering in Hailey's ear.

"You were saying, four. You wanted to make it four strikes." She placed her hand on my thigh, dangerously close to my balled-up socks.

I swept my lips across her collarbone again.

"Five," she exhaled.

"Six," I muttered into her jawline.

"Seven," she whispered, squeezing my thigh and sending a spark straight through my veins and into my cock. It grew hard, straining against my ridiculously tight leggings, as if, at any moment now, it would burst out of the seams and wiggle its way over to her.

Ello!

"Eight." I raised my mouth to hers and gazed into her eyes.

She nodded back at me, parting her lips and inviting me in. I wasn't gentle anymore. I savagely took her mouth, pressing into her and knocking us against the back of the booth. We didn't come up for air until the band stopped playing.

"See, cupcake, you're not bad. You're just drawn that way." I put my arm around her and pulled her close, nestling my nose into her wig.

"That's my line. And we can't keep doing this. Every time I see you, this happens."

"Raw animal magnetism."

"It's not animal magnetism. It's you putting the moves on me!" She took a deep breath, nearly popping out of her plunged neckline.

"But you asked!"

"I didn't! I said, four. Or five. Or something. I was counting." She pulled the cocktail straw out of her drink and took a long sip, wetting her lips and washing the taste of me away.

"So, what? You're giving me math lessons? Because it sounded like you wanted me to keep going." I pulled back from her, checking her expression. I didn't want to cross any boundaries.

"Fine. I did. But I can't be fraternizing with the enemy. And I'm fragile right now. I'm fresh out of a relationship!" she said.

"With the dildo I saw you with the other day? The man, not the one in your purse. Tall, lanky, breath smelled janky? That asshole?" My nostrils flared at the thought of him grabbing her.

"Yeah, that asshole."

"I don't want to know his name. The way he touched you tells me all I need to know about him. Don't pay him any damn attention. You're here with me now," I said.

"Exactly. I'm here with you—public enemy number one. My parents raised me to hate anyone with the last name Moretti, you know." Her thick lashes fluttered down to the empty glass in her hand.

"I know. I was raised to hate anyone with the last name Simmons. But I'm not my family, and I think you have the wrong idea of me. I'm sorry if I came on strong. I don't mean to offend you."

"Oh, shush. You didn't offend me. You know I liked it. I can't hide it. If you were anyone else, I would jump your bones out in the parking lot." She let out an exasperated sigh.

"Really?" I tilted my head toward her and lowered my voice. "But I'm not Dominick Moretti. I'm the Goblin King."

"Then, I guess it's okay!" She threw her hands in the air.

"Damn, that was easy. Too easy. Are you pranking me? Is this some type of trap?" I scanned the room for other members of BAD who might jump on me at any moment, put a bag over my head, and take me to some unknown destination—and hopefully bang me.

Damn, I need to stop watching so much porn.

"No, not a trap. But mention this to anyone and—"

"Snitches get stitches. Got it." I slapped a hundred on the table and hopped out of the booth, pulling her up after me. Her body brushed against mine, and I knew I needed to run. These leggings hid nothing.

I couldn't believe what was happening. One minute, Hailey Simmons had seemed ready to strike me down, and the next, she had admitted that she wanted to jump my bones. If she wasn't trouble by name, she was trouble by actions. A woman like her could flip-flop the fuck out on me if I wasn't careful. Been there, done that.

"I have a Jeep. It might smell like Sanchez. But ... I guess I wasn't prepared for this sudden turn of events." I led her to my car, which I'd parked far away from the others. I didn't want my new ride to get dinged up by drunken freshmen.

"That's rule number three in the BAD house: always be prepared." She opened her clutch and pulled out a condom, slipping it into my palm.

When she'd mentioned jumping my bones, I hadn't thought she meant sex. I'd thought we'd head back to my Jeep, and I'd slip my tongue down her throat, maybe suck a nipple or two. I'd hoped her hand would mosey down my pants, maybe her mouth.

"Hailey, I ..." I started. I paused beside my car, running my hand through my mullet wig.

"What? Is something wrong? Unlock the door! Someone will see us! Do you have any idea how many followers I have? They're everywhere!" She turned, looking around the parking lot.

"No. I just wasn't expecting to have sex with you, is all." I unlocked the door and hoisted her into the backseat.

"When you say you weren't expecting this, are you stalling because you see me as a respectable woman, or do you mean, you didn't prepare, as in trim your triangle?"

"My triangle? Good grief! I laser anyway. Who uses razors anymore? But that's beside the point. Of course I see you as respectable." I hopped in beside her, shutting and locking the door.

"Respectable women like to fuck too," she said.

"Yeah, they do." I smirked, but my smile faded when I lifted my gaze to her scowl.

"So, you don't want to fuck me? Great! You aren't the first one. I think I'll go now." She gathered up her dress in her fists and tried to push past me.

I held up a hand, stopping her. "Hold on now. I never said that. I was just sayin'—" I started.

"Then, fucking do it. You might be a Moretti, but I'm a Simmons. Don't underestimate me. I get what I want too. Always." She placed her palm on my chest and pushed me back into the seat before lifting her dress and climbing onto my lap.

I gritted my teeth. My heart hammered against my chest as her hips wiggled across my leggings. She moved back and forth, straddling the wadded-up socks in my underwear. I pulled the dress down her shoulders, exposing her perky, round breasts sitting snug in a strapless bra. I reached around her back, trailing my hand up her spine, and unclasped it. She threw it to the side and flashed me the most perfect pair of breasts I'd ever seen. She'd probably gone to Dr. Hatch. All the ladies of Forks used him.

I put my lips around one of her puckered nipples, sucking it between my tongue and teeth before coming up for air. She threw her head back and rubbed against me harder. Her fiery-red wig almost matched the flush spreading across her chest. I put my palm around her neck and pulled her to me, gently digging my fingertips into her throat. I pushed my mouth on hers and groaned while she slid back and forth in a steady rhythm.

I reached down to pull my fake balls out, ridding myself of my stupid, cramped pants, when bright headlights swept over my Jeep, distracting me from the task at hand. I stopped, craning my neck around Hailey to make sure they were gone. They weren't. My dad's Aston Martin turned around and was headed right for us.

"Fuck!" I set Hailey aside and pushed her down on the floorboard. "Get down. Cover up with this." I reached back for a blanket from the pile I kept for when I took Sanchez to the dog park.

"What is it? And why does this blanket smell like a wet dog?" She gagged.

"Shh." I pressed the button on the backseat and pushed it back to give us a little more room. "My dad." I threw another blanket over myself and crouched beside her.

"Oh no," she whimpered. "He's going to whack me! I just know it!"

"He's not going to fucking touch you."

Headlights flooded my Jeep, and the steady roar of his engine idled, sending a low vibration throughout my backseat.

"This was dangerous. I knew coming here was dangerous. You're dangerous," she whispered over the hum of my dad's car.

"I'm trying to change all that. Don't you see?" I bit back.

My dad revved his engine again, vibrating my Jeep from only a few feet away.

"You can't change who you are," she said.

"Because I share the same last name as my dad, people have this perception of me that I'm like him. He's a grade-

A asshole with zero redeeming qualities. I don't know what exactly he did to your dad, but that's on him. Not me. All I can say is, I'm not like him, and I was hoping you'd see that in me. For goodness' sake, I want to save cats and shit!" I whispered, straining my words until my throat burned.

"What? Save cats? Are you, like, PETA or something?" she asked.

"No, I'm not PETA or something. I'm going to veterinary school!"

"Huh? You're not carrying on the architectural firm? You're the only one in line to inherit it, right? That's a billion-dollar business. What's wrong with you?" Her voice rang out in a high-pitched shrill.

"Thanks for the support," I muttered.

The sudden wave of heat under these covers was stifling.

"I'm sorry. I didn't mean it in a bad way. Saving animals is a very noble job. Kinda cute actually. But all the money you're giving up … that's a lifetime of little worries."

"Says who? My dad hates his job. He's miserable and constantly stressed. Money only makes people crazy. Case in point, whatever he did to your dad. I heard they were best friends. Do you know the details?"

"No, only that your dad stole my dad's business plans," she said.

"Huh. That's all I know too."

My dad revved his engine again before putting his car in reverse and backing away. The headlights and rumbling sound of his exhaust slowly faded into the distance.

"I'm going to take a peek. Sit tight." I threw the covers off, took a deep breath, and poked my head up. I peered out the windows and saw nothing. "It's clear. You can sit up," I said, helping her off her knees.

"Phew. I'm glad he didn't realize we were in here," she said, brushing dirt off her dress.

"Oh, he knew. That was a warning." I curled my fist and wondered if my old man would ever let me be.

"Really? How ... sociopath." She flinched, darting her eyes around the parking lot.

"He only gets this way when it comes to your family. I don't know why. I need to get to the bottom of it. Maybe you can do some digging, too, and we can figure this out." I rolled my tense shoulders, mentally cursing my cockblocking father.

"I don't know. I was scared, Dominick. I'm not sure you and I talking or doing whatever we were about to do is such a good idea. I think I just want to go home."

I nodded. I'd wanted her to feel secure and safe with me, not threatened. So much for shaking my bad reputation.

"I'll drop you off at your car. I'm sorry, Hailey. Maybe it is better if we let things cool down," I said in a voice as low as I felt.

She pulled her dress up over her breasts and tucked herself away. I handed her bra to her and climbed in the front seat.

"How did he know we were here anyway? Did you tell anyone?" she asked, adjusting her wig.

"Nope. Did you?" I turned my key in the ignition and pulled away.

"Only Madison. But she's my best friend. She wouldn't tell a soul. My ride's over there, by the way." She pointed to a white Audi at the other end of the parking lot.

"And you're sure she wouldn't gossip?"

"I'm positive. Snitches get stitches. And us BAD girls know how to stitch. Doesn't mean we'll be stitching anyone up though. We're more the type to leave our perpetrators to bleed out. Especially Madison. Preston had better watch himself." She laughed.

"Yeah, I'm aware of them two," I said, pulling in beside her car. I turned back around and squeezed her knee, trying to lighten the dark mood that had spoiled the night.

"I had a good time tonight even though my skin smells like a wet dog and I squatted in something mushy and questionable back here on your floorboard. Before drama went down, it was nice. I … liked it." She tugged her lavender gloves off one by one and scooted toward the door.

"I did too, Hailey. Maybe in another life." My voice wavered. I tried to smile, but my face fell flat.

"In another life," she sighed. A smile spread across her cheeks but stopped right below her empty eyes. She pushed the back door open and jumped out of her seat. "It's only forever, Dominick. That's not long at all," she said before closing the door and getting in her car.

I stayed until she disappeared out of sight and out of my life.

HAILEY

I woke up early Saturday morning to catch my dad before he hit the golf course. From the earliest I could remember, my dad had spent every Saturday releasing work tension with his buddies through several rounds of golf. My very traditional mother would cook him an elaborate breakfast and have dinner on the table when he came back home. I'd always wished he would invite me when I was younger, but my mom had taught me that he needed time to decompress from his hectic career.

His clients were demanding and expected him to be available at any time during the day. He even frequently received calls after work hours. I'd never known the business of building homes for the elite was as stressful as it was until I saw the way my dad's jaw was set tight at the dinner table evening after evening. Dominick had said his dad was stressed all the time, too, but at least his dad hadn't had his business plans stolen out from under him and been forced to take on a smaller and less prestigious career path. My dad had been fighting an uphill battle ever since.

So it goes anyway.

I hit the security code at the entrance of my old neighborhood and pulled through the iron gates. Nothing changed in suburbia. We were still as basic as ever. The homes were carbon copies of each other, the lawns all manicured precisely, and even the homeowners rarely moved away. In the fifteen years we had lived here, I only remembered one family moving out of our cul-de-sac. The rest just grew old and withered in their comfortable and safe bubble.

As I turned the corner to my parents' house, I spotted Mrs. Peters walking her three Chihuahuas up ahead. The sight of those little dogs instantly reminded me of Sanchez—and Dominick, as if he hadn't been on my mind all last night and this morning already. Dominick was the only reason I'd set my alarm to wake up and visit my parents.

I hadn't been able to fall asleep last night. The thrill of our sexcapades and the anxiety of his dad's threat sent adrenaline coursing through my veins until well past midnight. I tossed and turned and even broke out my magic vibe. But still, I couldn't sleep. It wasn't until I'd decided to wake up early and drive to my parents' house when I finally closed my eyes and drifted off into a restless slumber.

I had no idea how I would investigate our families' drama without seeming suspicious. One mention of Louis or the Moretti dynasty, and my dad would prickle. I never brought up the drama, but I'd seen others attempt it in passing. It never ended well. Once, I'd tried to ask my mom about his hatred of them, but she'd only told me to count my blessings and say my prayers. She'd told me a good churchgoing man like my dad hated no one. He only disliked their sinful nature.

But even I could tell that was a lie she forced herself to swallow. And after Dominick's dad's psycho threat last night, I could see where he was justified to dislike the Morettis.

I pulled into our expansive driveway, past the stone lampposts, and right behind one of my dad's many vintage cars. For someone to be so upset over a stolen business opportunity, I didn't think we had much to complain about in life. Finances were never an issue. We were blessed, as my mother would say.

I got out of my car just as my dad opened the garage and began dragging out his golf bag.

"Hey, Dad!" I called out, startling him.

His brow hung over his hollow eyes, and his graying hair stood out on all ends, as if he hadn't slept last night either.

He jumped, zipped his bag, and turned toward me. His face was thin and his eyes bloodshot. I recognized his expression from the many times he had to work late, dealing with asshole clients.

"Hey there, kiddo! What're you doing here?" He held out his arms and embraced me, holding me tight.

I was my dad's only child and admittedly a daddy's girl. My mom and I tended to butt heads, but my father and I always got along just fine.

Of course, I never let him down. I hadn't rebelled in my teen years or caused any issues for the family. I went to school, did my work, and came home to do whatever was expected of me. Usually, that was chores, church, and studying. I was a good girl, and a plain, boring, innocent lady—the most basic of the basic. I knew nothing else.

"Sorry to pop over without calling. I didn't know I'd come until late last night. I just got a little homesick, I guess." I shrugged, brushing my hair from my eyes.

My mother had recoiled in horror when she saw I'd dyed my locks pink. She'd clicked her tongue in distaste for months until my visits became less frequent. My dad never mentioned it, though I was sure my colorful decision didn't fit into his traditional family portrayal.

"You can pop over anytime. We'd love that. Run inside. Your mom's got breakfast on the table. I'm going to put this bag in my trunk, and I'll be right there." He wiped his brow and gave a dismissive wave of his hand, shooing me inside.

"Okay," I said, turning away to obey and dutifully run along without question.

I hadn't seen my dad in months, but again, he was a busy man. Always.

I opened the door and made my way to the kitchen, following the smell of bacon and my mom's famous fried potatoes. I dragged my feet down the corridor, pausing to smile and reminisce over the vacation portraits hanging on the walls. There were photos of us at the beach, at a pizza parlor in Italy, and on a train in France. But my personal favorite was when we stood next to a geyser in Yellowstone.

We hadn't expected the blowhole to erupt while we were nearby. The park ranger had told us the chance of seeing an active eruption was very slim. But when my parents strolled by and the geyser spouted off, their faces were priceless. I'd snapped a smiling selfie of me with my parents laughing in the background and the fountain shooting out of the frame. There wasn't a trace of stress on anyone's face.

Other trips had been fun, too, but an underlying tension always crept into my dad's moods. Which then crept into my mom's mood and then into mine. When he was alive, even our old dog, Rambo, had seemed to turn sour when my dad had a bad day.

"Hailey?" My mom's face lit up. She tapped her spatula on the edge of the pan before setting it aside and throwing her arms around me. "Is something wrong? You're never here this early or much at all anymore." She kissed me on the top of my head before holding me at arm's length and awaiting my answer.

"Nothing's wrong. I just got homesick." I gave a halfhearted smile and ignored her sneaky guilt trip.

"That's when you know you've raised 'em right, Carol. They come back," my dad called from behind me.

"Bless your heart, sweet girl. You can stay however long you'd like. Is everything all right at school? Come and sit at the table. Eat." She pushed me toward a chair and began to make a plate of food.

"Just bacon. No potatoes, please! I'm watching my carbs. I have to be in top shape for the fashion show. The theme is Merry Fit-mas. Or something like that. Madison wants to brand a line of fitness clothes, so naturally, she's promoting herself."

My dad pulled out a chair and sat beside me. His plate was piled high with fried potatoes, bacon, and scrambled eggs. My stomach let out a rumbling growl.

"She's going places. I'll give her that. Both she and her mother have the entrepreneurial attitude you need in this world. Eat or get eaten," my dad said, smacking his lips as he chewed.

"Or marry a rich man and divorce him, as Ms. Sheffield did, isn't that right, Walter?" my mom asked, turning and raising her eyebrows at my dad.

She set a plate of bacon and a cup of orange juice in front of me. I always knew my mom didn't care for Madison's mom's lifestyle choices. I chalked it up to Liza Sheffield living freely and doing as she pleased. My mom never even thought for herself. If God or her husband didn't tell her to do something, she wouldn't do it. She answered to no one else.

"That works." He laughed. "Prenup. You'll sign one, too, one day. Not for whoever you choose to marry, but to protect yourself. I can't have some guy running off with all my—your—assets," my dad said. He stabbed at his potatoes, piercing them with his fork and popping them into his mouth.

"I'll always protect what's mine. You taught me that, Dad. I'm cautious. Which is kind of why I wanted to come here today." I massaged the back of my neck.

"I thought you were homesick," my mom said, sitting down beside me with a fruit plate. She ate like a bird and looked like one too. Her diet consisted mainly of sweet tea and prayers.

"That too. But …" I stammered, shifting my eyes to the fountain just outside of the kitchen window.

"You found someone. Who's the lucky guy?" My dad leaned forward and pushed his empty plate aside.

"No. I haven't found anyone. It's not like that. But I did run into someone." My voice caught in my throat. I took a sip of my drink and continued, "His name is Dominick … Moretti."

My dad lifted his chin and curled his lips. "And? Did he have anything to say? Is there something you want to ask us?"

My mom fidgeted with the napkin on her lap. Her eyes widened as she looked back and forth from my dad to me.

"Nope. Nothing. I just ran into him, is all. I said hi, and he did too. I'm not sure he knew who I was. I didn't even know who he was until one of the sorority sisters told me afterward. I was just letting you know." I shrugged, biting off a piece of greasy bacon and choking it down.

"I'm glad you told us. And I'm glad you left it alone. They're dangerous. Stay away from that family." He pushed himself from the table and brought his plate to the sink, tossing it in before turning to leave. "I'm going to be late for the tournament."

I looked to my mom, but she only shook her head, silencing me from further speaking on the topic.

"Okay, Dad. Good luck today!" I called, but he was already down the hall.

I waited until I heard the door shut before I pressed my mom for answers. She leaned back in her chair, closed her eyes, and rubbed the bridge of her nose between her index finger and thumb.

"What did I do?" I asked.

"You know you can't mention that family in this house. Your dad wants the best for you and our family. The Morettis aren't it. As he said, they're dangerous."

"But how do you know? How dangerous? Like, *bury me in their backyard* dangerous? Or *steal my work* dangerous? Or *hurt my feelings* dangerous?" I pressed.

"All of the above There's a reason your dad keeps us separate from them."

"Okay, what's the reason? I only know rumors—they were best friends once, and Louis stole from Dad. Now, Louis is a billionaire, and we're millionaires. Gee, it doesn't sound too terrible in the long run." My nostrils flared. "I can't even so much as talk to their son, and I get anxiety. I don't know why! No one has told me why I should hate them. Good, churchgoing families don't hate. Especially ones as blessed as us."

My mom flinched. "We don't hate them. We just avoid them. You can't trust them. Your dad just so happens to know how bad they can be, and he doesn't want to associate with their scandalous behavior. It's beneath us."

"What if their son isn't like that? What if he's a really good guy? He's going to vet school, you know. To save animals and bring about world peace and all." I pushed my plate of bacon aside and folded my arms over my chest. I felt the thumping of my heart under my thin cotton blouse.

"I thought you'd only said hi to him." The blood drained from her face. She pursed her lips together in a thin line, stopping her bottom lip from trembling.

"I made small talk. I didn't want to tell Dad and upset him more. I saw a vein pulsing in his temple as soon as I mentioned Moretti. Dominick had seemed genuine, Mom. And I feel guilty for even saying that, but I don't know why. I shouldn't. It's like I was brought up and wired by you and Dad not to trust these people I don't even know anything about. All I know is, his dad stole my dad's plans ages ago. But I'd say, we're doing fine now. Where's this forgiveness you always preach?" I threw my hands in the air.

"It's not my place to discuss your dad's business."

She pushed herself up from the table and took her plate to the trash can, scraping her uneaten fruit into the garbage. The sound of her fork scratching against porcelain made the hairs on the back of my neck rise.

"Not your place? You're his wife and on equal ground as him. I'd say, it's your business too. Especially if there are these unspoken rules we have to live by, like, don't talk to a spooky Moretti." I rolled my eyes.

She slumped her shoulders forward and sighed. I hadn't meant to come across as harsh on my mother. She'd worked her ass off to give me the traditional, fundamental upbringing she thought was best. But she stood in the shadows of my dad, and whatever he said, she took for gospel. I didn't think that way at all. I was basic, as I had been brought up to be, but the last few years of college had exposed me to a different walk of life. Lately, I'd been questioning everything.

"Your father has always provided us with everything we need and everything we want. I don't question his choices because they've always been with family first in mind. I'm okay with letting him lead. He hasn't steered us wrong yet. That's just part of marriage."

"I don't think so. I think I'd prefer to have an equal partnership than have someone tell me how to act, think, and feel."

"Always thought a liberal school would brainwash you." She shook her head.

"What? You mean, teach me to form my own opinions?" I asked.

"Throw you to the wolves and undo all the protections we put in place to keep you safe. I told your dad this would happen. I knew as soon as you came home with that wild hair of yours."

I reached up, smoothing my hair down and behind my ears, as if I could hide it from her criticism.

"Wild hair? It's my hair, on my head, and I like it. I'm much less a lemming and much more my own person. My hair's just a reflection of that."

"I'm tired, honey. I think I'm going to lie down a bit. You can stay if you want, but I need to lie down." She leaned against the doorway.

"No, thanks. I've got work to do." I slid out of my chair and hugged her good-bye.

"Stay safe, Hailey. Please, use your head and be careful over there. Leave the Moretti boy alone," she said, squeezing my hand before letting me go.

"I'll be careful. I'll let myself out. Go lie down." I waved her away and quickly cleaned the kitchen, like the dutiful daughter she'd raised.

By the time I finished, Madison had texted me to come to the studio as soon as possible.

Great. What now?

I gathered my things and left, tiptoeing outside. When I turned to push the button to close the garage, I spotted my dad's set of golf clubs leaning against the wall, still shiny and looking as if he never used them.

I entered the design studio and took a deep breath, filling my lungs with the familiar air of coffee and hot irons on dyed fabric. This was my happy place. The low hum of the sewing machines lulled me into a relaxed state of mind. I spotted Madison leaning over a table covered with sketches. She stuck her foot out, shifting her weight from side to side. I rarely saw Madison sit. She preferred to pose, switching her angles every few minutes.

"And?" Madison asked without looking up from her work.

"And what?" I slid my bag on the table and picked up a sketch of a woman wearing high-waisted athletic pants and a strappy matching bra.

Madison rarely had terrible fashion sense. She was one of those rare prodigies with a passion for fashion and the talent to match.

The only time I could remember a flop from her was when she had tried to create a line of cat clothes for the local kitty shelter. Neither of us had experience with cats. When we wrestled this gorgeous Siamese feline into a fancy-pants dress, she clawed her way out and up Madison, perching on her head before jumping and snatching her wig.

I wouldn't have believed it either if I hadn't been there. Thankfully, no one else had seen that fiasco. Madison had sworn off cats and wigs ever since.

"And how did your date with the enemy go? You weren't in your room. Don't tell me you stayed at his place." She lifted her eyes to mine.

"Shh. Lower your voice," I said, scooting in closer to her. "No, I didn't stay there! I went to my parents' this morning. But my date was fine. More than fine. It was fun up until his dad threatened to ram into us with his car."

"What?" she gasped. "You don't say. If only there were warning signs that this was a bad idea and his family was dangerous."

"Ha-ha. Very funny. It was serious. I've never been put in a crazy, psycho situation before. Have you?" I picked up another sketch, inspecting the perfect lines she'd drawn.

"Besides the ones I create for myself, nope."

"Well, whatever. It's over. That was enough for both of us. We ended it on a good note, I think," I said.

"So, he won't reach out to you again?" She began separating her sketches into two different piles.

"Nope."

"You're sure about that?" she asked, drumming her fingers across the table.

"Yep." I lied—or pretended.

"Good. Moving on. I've settled on Diana, Shay, and Natalie for the recruits. I'm telling them all tomorrow at brunch, so you and Cheri are helping. Attendance is mandatory." She tapped on a sketch of a woman wearing what I thought was a stained cardboard tube top. "Is this sports bra too masculine? It's so hard to create a supportive bra without it looking like a shoebox."

"Yeah, it needs more work. I'll be there tomorrow, of course, but damn, I hate being the bearer of bad news. Who lost? I can't keep up with them this year. We had so many, but they seemed to dwindle toward the end. You must have scared them away."

"Speaking of, there's one now. Quick, turn around. I don't feel like small talk. I gotta get this fashion show underway." She grabbed my elbow and whirled me around, putting my back to the room.

I glanced over my shoulder. The recruit who walked through the door was the same lady in the pictures with Joel and Dominick. Her long, dark hair billowed out behind her like she walked around with a fan in front of her face, giving her the perfect couture photo opportunity.

"Fuck! Who's that girl? I saw her in photos with Dominick and Joel." I whispered.

Madison lowered her voice. "That's Jen Hathaway. She's a local model. She applied for BAD. Remember, she was one of the first to sign up this year? She isn't making it in though. She's a catty bitch. I mean, it's okay to have some bitch in you. We all do. But I draw the line when people start tearing others down, especially our own. She tried to bond with me during that first meeting. She scoffed at another recruit's boots. What the hell was she doing with Joel?"

"I have no idea." I felt Jen's gaze piercing me like a knife to my back. "But she keeps popping up all over the place. I guess I never paid attention until I saw her photo with Dom, but now, I know why she looked so familiar."

"She hasn't been participating much. She thinks she's too good and a natural shoo-in. The only thing she's a shoo-in for is a shoe in her ass. She even rolled her eyes when I mentioned the monthly giveback requirement. I told all of the candidates we volunteered once a month, and most of them nodded. Some smiled. Not this bitch. She rolled her eyes and twirled her hair."

"Where was I when all of this was happening?" I asked.

"Right beside me, duh! Your mind's been elsewhere." She raised her brow. "I swear, you're going to have to get it together. And now that both of your men are out of the picture, you can help me with the show. We'll work on it after we break the news tomorrow. Oh! And next weekend, Greek Row is having a block party to welcome all recruits across the houses. Everyone's participating, including us. Our table is serving desserts."

"But … that means he'll be there. I don't want to run into him." I took a sketch out of a pile and pretended to be interested, but again, my mind was elsewhere.

"If I can handle Preston being there, you can handle Dom. Besides, you said he was nice, and you two aren't talking anymore. So, just don't talk to him. I don't want to represent BAD without my best friend beside me."

"We don't even live on Greek Row though," I protested.

"We're still a part of the team," she said, holding up her phone camera and pushing out her lips. "Scoot in. I'm hashtagging how we're still working on a Saturday. Hashtag *boss babes*. It doesn't get any better than this."

"Yep. Doesn't get any better than this," I lied—pretended.

DOMINICK

Just two days ago, I'd hidden in the backseat of my Jeep from the man who now sat across from me. I focused on the flower arrangements on our antique mahogany table, the woven tapestry hanging behind my mother, and the yellowed chandelier casting a hazy light across our textured walls.

I'd successfully avoided my dad's gaze since I arrived an hour ago. He and I hadn't spoken a word, and my mother was too busy to notice the tension building.

I hadn't wanted to come to Sunday dinner, but she'd pressured me into making an appearance for our guests. My aunt Edna and uncle Ray were here, and my mother had wanted to create a special dinner for my aunt, who'd been diagnosed with Alzheimer's years ago. Her mental state had been steadily declining, but she kept her feisty attitude. She was still a Moretti to the core.

I watched as my mother threw back her wineglass and guzzled it down. When she came back up for air, she relaxed her shoulders and flashed me a plum-stained smile. She'd prepared four different dishes tonight, hoping one would suffice for my picky aunt Edna. But so far, everything Edna had touched was an abomination.

"Is this squirrel?" Aunt Edna asked, picking up a slice of veal and waving it at my ma. She stuck it in her mouth and smacked her lips.

"No, honey. That's veal. We don't eat squirrels," my mom answered, reaching over to pat her hand.

"Speak for yourself." Aunt Edna took another bite of veal.

My mother's eyes cut to mine when she noticed I was pushing the pasta around on my plate instead of gulping it down, as I usually did with her meals. She raised her brows at me and then my father. I wondered if she knew about my dad's antics last Friday night and how he'd threatened me with vehicular homicide. At least, I would play that card if I had to. I was a mama's boy, and my ma always stepped in to save me, even when I did dumbass shit.

I'd stolen one of our golf carts a few years back to impress my friends at the all-boys' school I attended. I only planned on driving it around and getting as reckless as doing a doughnut in the driveway. But those boys had other plans. They wanted to build a demolition ring in the woods behind our neighborhood. They grabbed a few other carts and decided we should spray-paint them to look like monster trucks. I knew what I was doing, but I was desperate to fit in even if it was with the wrong crowd.

I painted my golf cart black and called it *Dom*inator. I was proud until one of my friends invited some older guy named Weston, who lived nearby. Weston brought over a jacked-up purple golf cart with dice hanging from the ceiling. He called it the pussy wagon. One round in the demolition ring and the P-wagon destroyed my *Dom*inator. I had to push my mangled cart all the way home.

Fortunately, I usually wasn't a troublesome kid, like most of the rich punks I hung around. My ma took one look at the golf cart and had it taken away and trashed before my dad arrived back home from his trip. She replaced it with a newer, sleeker model and told him she felt he needed an upgrade.

La famiglia prima di tutto.

The other boys hadn't been so lucky.

Uncle Ray cleared his throat. "How's business, Louis?" He reached over and wiped a dribble of sauce off of his wife's chin.

My dad's jaw muscle twitched back and forth. "Business is business. The work never stops. How are things at the hospital?" he said, shoveling food into his mouth.

"This squirrel is so good. What's your name, dear? I'd like this recipe." Aunt Edna smiled a meaty grin.

"I'm your sister-in-law, Gabriella. You can call me Gabby. I'll fix you up some squirrel to take home." My mom winked, pouring herself another glass of wine. Her chest fell in a sigh of relief as she sat back and watched Edna chew her meal.

"The hospital's the same. Never a dull moment," Uncle Ray continued. "I completed a lung transplant last week that took twelve hours, but the patient is doing remarkably well. It's an amazing feeling, saving someone. I never get tired of it. I suspect you'll feel the same way in vet school, Dominick. Have you had any hands-on practice yet? Saved any lives?"

"I spend most of my time in labs or studying. But we have started to venture out to local farms to learn how to handle the animals. We helped deliver baby sheep last week." I put my fork down, clinking it against the fine china my mother only used when guests dined with us.

Aunt Edna gasped. "I knew this tasted like sheep!" She pushed her plate away and made the sign of the cross.

"No, it's not sheep. It's squirrel, remember?" Uncle Ray patted her shoulder and scooted her plate back in front of her.

She looked at it and shrugged before gulping another bite down.

"I got my eye on you," Aunt Edna said between mouthfuls, wagging her bony finger at me.

"Everyone does," I muttered into my wineglass.

My father held his drink in his hand and took a long sip before clearing his throat and addressing my uncle, "Saving animal lives is different than human lives. I'm not sure my son would get the same level of satisfaction you do, Ray. They're just animals. They're more trouble than they're worth." He set his drink down and peered at me.

"It's a noble calling. All of God's creatures. So, he wants to save animals. We should count our blessings. He could have wanted to be a lawyer." My mom laughed while shooting the evil eye at my dad.

I kicked my foot back and forth across the thick Persian rug underneath me and took another sip of wine.

"You know, what I like is the dangerous animals. Maybe it's the thrill of it. I don't scare easily. No matter how threatening the animal can be, I'm able to handle it." I took the napkin off my lap and set it on the table.

"Squirrels are dangerous. You have to bop them upside the head quick." Aunt Edna curled her hand into a fist and smacked it with her other palm before dragging her index finger across her throat. "Isn't that right, Gladys?" She nodded at my mom.

"You're absolutely right." My mom grabbed her knife and placed it further from Aunt Edna's reach.

"When you're out there, saving your animals, just be careful you don't step on a snake." My dad's voice came out as thick and slow as molasses.

"I think I'm observant enough to know a snake when I see one." I swirled my glass and threw back the last of my wine.

"Cake! I baked a cake! Who wants dessert?" My mom clapped her hands together and began to clear the table.

She grabbed Aunt Edna's plate, but my aunt's wrinkled hand shot out from under the table, stopping my mom.

"Are you trying to take my squirrel?" Aunt Edna growled.

"Nope," my mom said, patting Aunt Edna's hand. "I'll go get the cake."

"I'll help!" I pushed myself out from the table and followed my mom to the kitchen.

She set a stack of plates in the sink and leaned against the granite countertop, fanning her arms out and hanging her head.

"Ma? You okay?" I asked.

"No. I could cut the tension in there with a knife! What did you do?" She exhaled a loud breath through her nose.

"Me? Why did I have to do something? It's not me. It's him! He tried to crash his car into mine."

I threw my shoulders back and crossed my arms. She'd never taken his side before.

"Your father would never hurt you! I know you two don't get along, but he isn't going to kill you. Jeez, Dom! Use your head." She disappeared into the pantry, returning with a jar of sprinkles.

I took the glass dome off of the cake pedestal and pushed the cake toward her. My mother only put sprinkles on cakes for four-year-olds and Aunt Edna.

"Your dad trying to kill you," she muttered, shaking her head. "Ha!"

"I was at a bar—with Hailey Simmons." I lowered my voice.

She lifted her eyes to mine.

"I—"

She held up a hand, silencing me.

She tore the cap off the sprinkles and began shaking it over the cake. Colored dots flew across the countertop and scattered across the floor.

"I told you to stay away from her, and you didn't listen. That family is dangerous, see? Now, look at the trouble you're in."

"See what? The only danger I experienced was Dad's car pulling up to mine like he wanted to ram into us."

"So, you were in the Jeep with her?" She slammed the jar on the table.

"Yeah, I was. I'm a grown man, Mom. I can make out with a woman in my Jeep."

"Not that woman."

"Or the last one either, apparently. You and Dad hated Jen too."

The blood drained from my mother's rigid face.

"We're keeping you safe and on the right track, is all."

"I can make my own choices, thanks," I muttered. "You know, it's always drama with us. It makes me want to jump in my car and run away. I've never fit into this lifestyle and maybe even this family. This just isn't me." I waved my hands at the marble floor and the crystal chandelier hanging above the island.

"You've always been a part of this family." She put her arms around my shoulders and hugged me. "But you're making a big mistake, Dom. Your dad and I won't budge on this. You'll have to stay away from the girl or run away. See how far you can get. It's a tough world out there, my love. I know you've always gotten everything you've ever wanted, but you can't have her. Sorry, son." She looked up at me with tears in her eyes.

I'd seen my dramatic mom cry plenty, but I'd never felt her words weigh as heavy as they did with grief. I knew she wanted me to be happy, but I also knew there was a lot she wasn't telling me.

"I'm not hungry anymore, Mom. I'll say my good-byes and leave. I have a lot of studying to do. Thanks for dinner. I love you." I leaned in, kissing her forehead.

She pressed her lips together and nodded.

I told everyone good-bye and hurried out the door, slamming it shut behind me. I didn't want to be here or anywhere near the stress and drama revolving around this elitist lifestyle forced upon me. The days of my dad pushing me around were over.

Veterinary school wasn't exactly how I'd pictured it to be. I had known I would have to deal with some emotional shit in this industry, but I hadn't been prepared to experience some of the things I'd learned in my short time here. When it came to my soft spot for animals, I had to toughen up fast.

A student had brought a box of injured baby rabbits into the clinic earlier in the week. I nursed them for days, but they showed no improvement. They were beyond saving. Yesterday, I held two of them while they passed away in my palms. The only thing I could offer was the warmth and care in my hands. I trudged home late last night and fell asleep in a downward spiral of hopelessness.

I'd woken up with renewed energy only because today was the Greek Row barbecue, and I'd surely get to see Hailey there. If anything could break me out of my week of despair, it was her. I hadn't seen or heard from her since the night my dad scared her away. I knew it was best if I didn't reach out, and if she wanted to keep seeing me, she would let me know. But I never received any texts from her after '80s night. She'd set her boundaries.

The DIK house was in charge of grilling brats for the party. Leave it to Preston to pick the lewdest items available as a joke. He'd already made a tablecloth with an *Eat a DIK* slogan. Our stereotype as the notorious bad-boy pranksters who continually got away with antics was on the nose. We weren't the preppiest fraternity or the biggest partiers. We definitely weren't the smartest or the classiest. But we were the wealthiest, and that made us the most powerful.

"Ready for the Triple B, bruh?" Preston asked.

He followed behind me with a keg on a cart as I wheeled the grill to the front. Rows and rows of white-clothed tables lined the middle of our blocked-off street. Each house had its lawn decorated and their serving stations out on their driveways.

"Triple B?" I asked, craning my neck to see if I could spot BAD's setup.

"Beer, babes, and booty." He grunted, setting the keg down beneath our table.

"Ah, no. I haven't thought about it much. I'm still trying to declutter my brain from classes this week." I stretched my arms over my head and turned my face toward the sun.

The arctic blast we'd had not long ago left Forks with crisp, perfect autumn weather. The leaves on Greek Row's massive oak trees were just starting to turn their brilliant shades of color.

"Exactly. Beer, babes, and booty will help you relieve tension. I do it all the time, especially before a big exam. Studying has never worked for me. Instead, I grab a beer, some ass, and bust a nut. I don't know how to describe it. It's like an epiphany, I guess. The clouds part, and the gods smile down on me with their infinite wisdom." He clasped his hands together and shook them in the air at his invisible magic sex deity.

"So, you pass the tests?" I asked.

"Nope, but it sure beats studying. You should try it. The best time to dip your toes into FU's finest is the new-recruit barbecue. Do you have any idea how many young, inexperienced, first-year college students will be here? They flock to our station." He patted the *Eat a DIK* banner draped across our table.

"Why?" I scratched my head. "I don't think we can compete with some of these other stations."

The serving station belonging to the sorority across the street had a fancy cocktail setup, complete with what looked like a champagne fountain. The sorority sisters, dressed in all pink, were hanging streamers, tying balloons, and putting out flowers around their lawn. I hadn't ventured into getting to know all the houses on Greek Row yet, but I knew the house across the street—whatever their name was—were the *lady in the streets and freak in the sheets* type. Preston had bragged countless times about his affairs with those girls.

"Pfft. No one cares about that. It's because we have the money, and money gets us the Triple B. Everyone knows we're trust-fund babies. All you and I have to do is hold out a hand, and they'll put their ass into it." He clapped me on the back.

I scratched my jaw, cocking my head to the side. It had been a while since I'd had a lady grace my bed. I didn't need a woman, but I wanted one. Maybe the Triple B wasn't such a bad idea after all. As if Preston's magical sex deity had heard me, a group of BAD girls, including Hailey, walked out of the sorority across the street.

"Fuck!" Preston stiffened. "She has to ruin everything. She probably picked that spot just to torture me." He lifted his chin to Madison, who sneered and gave a little wave. He halfheartedly waved back. "They're too good to live on this street but not too good to party." He blew out a breath. "Figures."

"You still mad about the dirty Sanchez trick?"

My eyes followed Hailey as she began setting up a table with the other sisters. She hadn't looked over my way once.

"That and all the other annoying things she's done. I stayed at her house almost every summer. Her brother and I basically lived on the lake behind her place. But Madison would always find a way to ruin the day." His voice rose to a high pitch. "*Mom, Seth and Preston ate all of my protein bars. Mom, Seth and Preston won't drive me to the mall. Mom, Seth and Preston are inviting girls over and taking them to the pool house. Mom, Mom,*" he whined.

"So, you're saying she's a bratty little sister?" I asked.

"The worst," he said through gritted teeth. "She knows she annoys me. She does it on purpose. I still owe her for that dirty Sanchez bullshit. I might have to visit her station later."

I prickled at the thought of Preston and the brothers anywhere near Hailey.

"Let's play it by ear," I said, dragging him back inside.

I glanced over my shoulder, but still, Hailey was ignoring me.

The tables scattered in the middle of the street went mostly unused. People mingled back and forth between the houses, settling in lawn chairs or on blankets. Preston had set the recruits up at the serving station while he and I managed the grill.

I kept my head down other than the occasional peep across the street to see if Hailey had noticed me. She hadn't. She stood behind the table with her sisters, handing out cookies and cupcakes decorated in their house colors—platinum and gold. One of my brothers had snuck over to swipe a cookie earlier and brought a few back. They were shaped in red-soled shoes, leopard-print handbags, and different intricately designed dresses. I bit the heel of the shoe and peered over the grill toward her table again.

"I don't think we need to make any more. Crowds are dying down, and people are returning to their yards. Now's the time for the Triple B threat, bro," Preston said, turning toward me. "Good luck. I'm peacing out to that artsy-emo sorority down the street. Daddy needs to show those masochists who's boss tonight. Want to come with?"

I switched the grill off and wiped a bead of sweat from my forehead.

"Nah. I'll probably study," I lied. "Good luck though. Go clear your head."

"Ten-four. You hear that, recruits?" Preston turned behind us and shouted at the freshmen circling the keg. "Clean up. Leave the keg out. Everything else gets put up. Then, you can relax. Good job today. Welcome to DIK and welcome to the Row." He held his arms out, backing away and smiling before turning to jog off in the direction of the Triple B.

I helped the brothers wheel the grill back behind the house and take the station down before I poured myself a beer and settled into a lawn chair. Some recruit next to me was going on and on about his Physics course, but I drowned him out. I stared across the street, finally catching Hailey's eye. She quickly looked away before glancing back at me. I could see her chest rise and fall from where I sat. She stepped out from behind the table with Madison. They both held their phones out, taking selfies with their station in the background.

I couldn't tear my eyes from her if I wanted to. She stuck her leg out, posing in a skirt so short that if the wind blew the wrong way, I'd surely get a peek of what lay beneath.

"Blow, wind. Blow," I muttered.

"What was that?" the recruit asked.

"Oh, nothing. Sorry. Go on. Physics?"

The brother droned on and on in one long sentence, lulling me into a sleepy trance.

Madison threw her head back and laughed, mid-selfie. Hailey's eyes cut to mine again, and this time, she smiled.

My breath caught in my chest. I tapped my fingertips across my knee, twitching, aching, needing to feel her buttery skin underneath them. She snapped her eyes to me and bit her bottom lip with the familiar *come fuck me* expression all women tended to make when they flirted.

"Hold that thought. I have to take care of something." I pushed myself up from the chair and marched toward Hailey, leaving my brain back at the DIK house.

Her *come fuck me* expression changed into a *what the fuck are you doing* expression when I reached the midpoint between us. But I couldn't turn around now; my feet—and my dick—wouldn't let me. Her jaw dropped as she looked from left to right, scanning for anyone paying attention. Madison pushed her shoulders back and stiffened next to her.

"Do you have any cookies left?" I called out before I reached her table, hoping she would say no and I could turn around and save face. But the stack of cookies piled in a heap right in front of me said otherwise. "Err, I see you do. What I meant was, can I have one?" I grinned, sidling up to her table.

"I do. Let me get one for you," Hailey said, turning away from me and whispering to Madison.

Madison peered over Hailey's shoulder, narrowing her eyes at me before leaving in a huff.

"Ah, the Moretti curse. It's hit or miss. Some women throw themselves at me. Others kick me in the balls before I can introduce myself." I nodded toward Madison as she walked away, flipping her long hair behind her. "Which one will it be for you today?"

"Right now, I'd like to kick you in the balls. You know we can't be seen together," she whispered, speaking fast. "Ahem! What can I get for you, sir?" she said a little too loudly.

"Shh. You're the one drawing attention to us," I whispered. "I'll take a cookie, please, ma'am," I answered loud enough for the entire yard to hear.

"I need them to know you're just here for a cookie!" she whispered.

"I am just here for a cookie!"

She wrinkled her nose and began piling a stack of desserts on a plate before shoving it into my hands.

"Thank you!" I yelled.

"You're welcome, stranger!" she yelled back.

"Stranger? That's so obvious!" I whispered. "Would you like a sausage?" I called before lowering my voice back to a whisper. "Please?"

She wrung her hands and took a deep breath. "Yes, I would like an Italian sausage!" she replied in a high pitch.

"It's brats. Not Italian sausage! Unless you want some of this Italian sausage? Know what I mean?" I wiggled my brows in her direction.

The corners of her mouth twisted into a smirk. "Lead the way to the sausage party."

I shook my head and stuffed a cookie in my mouth to keep from laughing.

We crossed the street, both looking around for watchful eyes. Luckily, everyone was too drunk or too stoned to pay attention to what we were doing. Once we made it to the table of food, I set my cookies down and began to prepare her a plate. I knew she didn't want to be seen with me, and I didn't want to make her uncomfortable. I only wanted her to linger next to me long enough for me to breathe in her candy scent again.

"Thanks for the food. I've been working the station the whole time. I haven't gotten a chance to eat yet. Can't eat the cookies or cupcakes. Carbs aren't my friends," she said.

"You look as delicious as these cookies taste. You don't need to watch your carbs. I've seen and felt your body. It's perfect. I can't stop thinking about it, to be honest with you. I know it's dangerous, Hailey. But"—I lowered my voice and leaned into her—"meet me behind the DIK house. There's a wooden shed at the very back. I'll cause a distraction. If you sneak behind the cars in the drive, you can get there without being seen."

Our neighboring fraternity had packed up and snuck back inside. They were a brotherhood of engineers, techies, and lab rats—or according to Preston, nerds. They froze at the mere thought of the Triple B and much preferred to avoid social situations or anything that could make them stutter themselves into embarrassment—i.e., women. Preston used to give them a hard time until he began paying a few of the brothers to do his papers. Now, he mostly left them alone. Mostly.

"We're going to get caught," she whispered out of the side of her mouth.

"See you in a minute." I winked before handing her the brat.

She took the plate from my hand and marched back to her table. Her pink curls bounced with each click of her heels.

I ran inside and grabbed Sanchez, apologizing to him for being a pawn in our game. He didn't seem to mind. Last time, he'd had a bone twice his size, and this time, he could visit his best friend, who conveniently milled about down the street. Sanchez's best friend, Howie, was a short, chunky corgi. He stood twice as long and was twice as fat as Sanchez. When the two of them got together, they were trouble. Their energy fed off each other—in the competitive, stereotypical frat-boy behavior they'd learned from their masters.

I made it back outside and placed Sanchez on the sidewalk in front of the house. Almost immediately, I heard a howl down the street. Sanchez was usually a very well-behaved dog. He didn't jump on furniture, bark incessantly, or poop on the rugs. But one call from his best friend, and this little mutt reverted back to puppy mode.

Sanchez howled back at the corgi before taking off down the street in a pitiful attempt at running on his short legs.

"Ah!" I groaned. "Liam," I said to a recruit, "can you get him for me? I couldn't find the leash. I'll go check again."

Liam nodded, jogging off in Sanchez's direction. The barks and commotion from the two stunted mutts worked, even on me. When I managed to tear my gaze from the spectacle, Hailey had disappeared. I looked behind me and saw her pink hair bobbing through the windows of the parked cars. I jogged into the house, cutting through to the backyard and toward the shed. Sanchez's and Howie's excited barks echoed behind me.

"That was quite a distraction," Hailey said as soon as I made it to our hiding spot. "I hope poor Sanchez is okay. The other dog won't eat him, will he?" She fanned herself while leaning against the wooden shed and catching her breath.

"No. That's Howie. They're BFFs. He's fine." I laughed.

"I hope no one saw us. What do you think would happen if it got back to our parents?" She put her hands to her hips like she meant business, but the smile spreading across her face told me this was just another game.

"Ugh. Our parents! I'm so tired of the drama. Don't you ever get tired of it? All of this?" I gestured toward the fraternity houses. "This crowd. This stress. This lifestyle. Or do you like having everything handed to you on a silver platter?"

"It's all I know," she said, lowering her head and sighing.

"Me too. But that doesn't mean I'm forced to live it. You know, Hailey, this isn't me. This fraternity bullshit, the drama of whatever the fuck happens in our social circles, the putting on faces for social media, and the stuffy crowds. Half of them are fake and would turn their backs on me in a minute for a quick dollar. I'm just tired of it. Money really is the root of all evil." I ran my hands through my hair.

"Are you okay?" Her smile faded.

"I'm sorry. I didn't mean to come off as brash. Not sure where that came from. I'm having a hard time at Forks. I love what I'm doing at school, but I don't feel like I belong here. I never have and never will. And then this drama with our families is eating me alive. For my father to keep me— a grown man—from you, who has done nothing wrong … well, it's bullshit. I can't even get to know you. Look at us, sneaking around like teenagers!"

She pushed herself off the shed and stepped into me, circling her arms around my back and pulling me into a hug. My shoulders slumped forward as I wrapped my arms around her tighter. The tension melted off my body.

"I feel it too," she whispered. "I love what I get to do. I'm lucky—or blessed, as my mom would say. I can have the best of the best. But it's always for a price."

"Always. And I get the blessed line from my ma too."

"Well, we are. Sometimes, I go to the university café and see how the other students struggle, even to afford shitty cafeteria coffee. I have no idea how they can even pay for this expensive-ass school. I've never had to worry about tuition, food, or anything financial. That's one big stress we don't have. But I get what you're saying about the dramatic lifestyle and about fitting in. I'm pretty damn basic, normal, boring. I'm not like Madison with her trendsetting attitude or Cheri with her brazen behavior. I'm just me. That's why I dyed my hair like this. It was a last-ditch effort to stand out and … fit in." She shrugged, still holding on to me tightly.

"You're anything but basic, cupcake." I ran my hand up her back and into her pink curls, burying my nose in her signature sweet scent.

"Thanks, but I don't feel it. I understand where you're coming from though." She stepped back, lifting her eyes to mine. "It's like I'm not fulfilled. I work so hard, but I never accomplish anything meaningful. I'm not sure who I am. I think maybe I'm just who I was always told to be. It's crazy, isn't it? We both have this void, yet we have everything we could ever want!"

"Not everything." I brushed her hair from her face. My eyes fell to her lips, half-parted and waiting.

"Dominick?" Liam called from the backyard.

A group of brothers echoed my name behind him.

"Fuck!" I sighed. "If it's not our parents keeping us apart, it's the universe."

"It's okay. Go. In another lifetime." Her voice broke as she pulled away. She straightened her back and lifted her chin.

"I'm sorry, Hailey. But I'm not going to let you get caught. I'll distract the boys again, and you sneak away." I turned to leave.

"Dominick?" She stopped me.

"Yeah?"

"I've never shown that side of me to anyone. I'm always putting on a face and playing the part. I'm one of those fake people you mentioned." She hung her head. "I pretend a lot. Like I said, it's all I know."

"It's okay, Hailey. I won't tell anyone your secrets. But you don't have to pretend with me," I said, reaching for her hand.

"I won't because we aren't supposed to be seeing each other. It's too dangerous. Remember?"

"I know. I know." I took a deep breath, squeezed her hand, and left.

I steered my brothers back into the house, feeding them a bullshit line about looking for Sanchez's leash. Out of the corner of my eye, I spotted a flash of pink fly across the yard. Those few moments behind the shed hadn't been at all what I'd expected. I'd thought I would sneak another kiss or get to squeeze a boob. But instead, I'd gotten an intimate conversation and a peek into Hailey's vulnerable soul. She was just as lost in this world as I was.

I had to end the reckless behavior of getting close to her. Anyone could spot us together, twist the narrative, and destroy her reputation or what little good I had left of mine. I'd never forgive myself for that. If I was going to save the girl, I had to keep my distance and move on. I could pretend too.

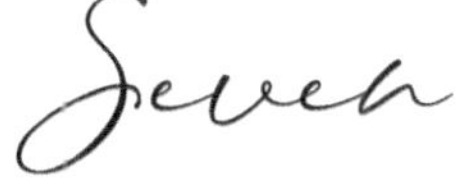

HAILEY

With Madison's help, I'd successfully maneuvered my way out of Dominick's life for the last three weeks. After the block party, I'd felt a sour change in me, and my best friend had sensed it too. We'd had Sunday brunch, posted social media stories, and spent hours in the design studio before she gathered the balls to call me out on my terrible mood.

"What's wrong with you? Ever since you gave Dominick that damn cookie, you've had space-cadet eyes!" Madison spun me around in front of the mirror before kneeling and adjusting my yoga pants.

We were the only two boss babes in the studio on the weekend.

"You'd better shape up! Both mentally and physically. The fashion show will be here before you know it, and you're modeling my brand! You know it's going to be formfitting, right? That means, no more late-night ice cream binges and put on a damn smile!"

"I know. I know," I echoed the last words I'd heard Dominick speak. A twinge of sorrow shot through my heart like a knife. "I like him, Madison. And I can't have him. I'm not used to not getting what I want. I tried mentioning him to my family, and they cut me off quickly. Whatever bullshit business deal had gone down, they won't even talk about it. He's not like the rest of them. He's got a heart."

"Look, you're my best friend. If you say he isn't a typical jackhole Moretti, I believe you. But I don't want to see you get hurt. The rumors about them being dangerous are scary. You even told me yourself about his dad meeting you at the bar! They are probably mobsters! But I'll do whatever it takes to help you, okay? Can we please just focus on this event for a while? It's a huge deal for me. I promise we can blow off some steam soon at the Halloween party. But until then, we need to focus. After this week, we should be all set to go as long as everyone keeps themselves in shape! I'm not going to constantly alter these damn clothes every time one of you bitches wants a pumpkin spice latte with extra whipped cream."

"Fine. I'll rein it in. But will you help me keep my mind off of him? Maybe I can do a spin class or a yoga class with you. I need a hobby," I said.

She pricked my butt with a sewing needle.

"Ouch!" I yelped, grabbing my ass.

"Oh, I'll keep your mind off him all right. Besides, I could do with a little break too. You're not going to want to hear this, but … we have a new model joining the team for the event. Diana can't make it. She's flying out that week. She asked if Jen could fill the spot. She'll be here for a fitting soon," she sputtered in one long mumble.

"What? You invited the stuck-up chick who's screwing my ex? I can't believe it!" I clenched my fists at my sides.

"We don't know if she's screwing your ex! You only saw a picture of them together!" she said, standing up and rolling her eyes.

"She was with Dominick too! And I've seen her everywhere lately. I had to use the toilet the other day in the middle of Visual Merch class, and she was there!"

"Where? In your class? Isn't she a first year?" She stuck the end of a few pins in her mouth and knelt back down, altering my pants at the ankle.

"No! In the toilet!" I said.

"In the toilet? What the fuck? Like, standing there? In a toilet?" she asked, spitting the pins out into her hand.

"Damn it, Madison! I mean, in the restroom. Look how flustered you got me." I pressed my palms deep into my eye sockets until I saw floaters.

"Just because she needed to use the restroom, I don't think that makes her a stalker. But she's still a bitch. For sure." She gathered the pins in her mouth again and went back to work.

"I didn't say she was a stalker. I never even knew her until this year. Besides, why didn't she go away after her rejection into BAD?" I asked.

"Some other sorority picked her up. She's still a student in design, and honestly, she has this modeling thing down to a T. I need this event to be as professional, perfect, and posh as possible. This is my future on the line!"

"Yeah, but inviting her is like me inviting Preston."

"What? They aren't even the same. Preston is the world's biggest shit stain. Jen's just an annoying shart," she said.

"It would make you just as uncomfortable though." I blew out a breath.

"You're going to be really uncomfortable if you don't drop about five pounds. You do know you're modeling my sports bras too? The fuchsia color is going to pop with your pink hair." She stood up, rustling my hair with her hand.

"Yeah, yeah. I'll get right on it. Just don't make me do any more events where Dominick will be there again. And keep me away from Jen too. When will she be here?" I asked.

"In about twenty minutes. I tried to keep you two apart. So, let's hurry and get this done, and you can be on your way and into the gym—not the campus gym. I've seen him there. See? I'm already on the mission to save you from his wretched grasp." She gave an over-the-top evil cackle.

"You're one in a million."

"Don't I know it!" She took a step backward to inspect her handiwork and gave herself a pat on the back.

To Madison's credit, she always performed a fantastic job when called to action. Since our little talk, I'd already lost three pounds and avoided stalking Dominick's social media page. I steered clear of the veterinary school building, the common campus areas, and Greek Row. I hadn't thought about him every second of the day, and I'd even had an enjoyable dinner with my parents, sans Moretti conversation.

There was a light at the end of the tunnel, and it pointed toward my bright future, which was why rule number one was rule number one. Besties came before testes, and I had let someone get in my way, knocking me off course for a bit, but I was back at it today even if I still felt slightly unfulfilled. I stuffed my void with what I knew and pretended I would be okay.

"You doing good?" Madison asked, breathless beside me.

She'd run three miles on the treadmill and only had a light sheen of sweat across her perfectly shaped brows. I wasn't as lucky as she was when it came to sparkling instead of sweating. I always left a workout, drenched. I had sweat circling my pits, under my boobs, down my crack, and even between my toes. I looked like a chewed-up piece of bubblegum next to this otherworldly creature. Madison had been born with more beauty and luck than I'd thought possible in one human being.

I pressed the button to make my machine go faster, determined to get my shit together—or at least look like I was trying.

"I'm getting there," I said between heaving breaths. "I feel like I'm dying."

"I meant, good with the moods. Not with the workout. You do look like you're dying." She sucked her breath in through her teeth and shook her head. "At least my workout gear is holding up though."

"Leave it to you to be more concerned about your clothing line than your dying friend." I patted the moisture-wicking yoga pants she'd sewn, which were surprisingly working.

"Hey! I did ask if you were doing good. Besides, I'm proud of you for even working out. This is the start of a new life for you. You got rid of your old baggage, and now, you're moving toward a future full of fashion, money, and men who are worth your time."

"I sure hope so. I feel like the only move I'm making right now is toward my grave," I croaked before climbing off the StairMaster and collapsing on a nearby bench.

"Okay, I guess that's enough for today. Let's grab lunch on the walk home." She hopped off the elliptical, did a few stretches, and sipped from her bedazzled water bottle before I could even stand on my shaky legs.

We walked back through campus because someone— not me—had had the bright idea to walk instead of driving our cars. Madison had said it would be an excellent warm-up and cooldown for our training. I'd agreed when we left the sorority house, but now, I was second-guessing myself. My feet dragged behind me like dead weight.

"Perk up, bitch. I'll buy you some tacos. Check it out. The Pink Taco Truck is here!" Madison tilted her chin up toward the taco truck.

Last year, The Pink Taco Truck had been a weekly habit, but this year, I'd been so occupied with school that I completely forgot about my favorite place. Which said a lot about my busy schedule because the women who worked the taco truck weren't quickly forgotten. They were loud, proud, and hilariously wild. If you were easily offended, The Pink Taco Truck wasn't for you. Thankfully, I was a BAD girl and loved their brazen behavior.

Just watching the ladies work together was the highlight of ordering off their menu. One woman would spout off the orders, cracking an invisible whip, and another would smack her on the ass with a dish towel. Meanwhile, the other two in the back would exchange jests and dirty jokes while whipping up some of the best damn tacos I'd ever had.

The first time we had eaten at the taco truck, I'd told Madison she should work with them because, with her attitude, she'd fit right into their girl gang. She'd contemplated it for a minute but ultimately decided it wasn't glamorous enough, and besides, she didn't need to work.

"Can you order me the naked tacos? The ones without the shells because stupid carbs," I asked Madison. "With extra Shizzle Sauce, please? I need to sit down. I don't think I can stand anymore."

"I got you," she said, skipping up to the order window.

I wobbled toward a picnic table underneath a giant oak tree, groaning as I swung each leg around the wooden bench and sat down. I scrolled through my phone until Madison came back with lunch. She bounced with each step, looking youthful, well-rested, and glowing.

"Thanks," I said, taking the food from her hands and scarfing it down to quiet my hangry stomach

"Uh, napkin?" Madison held out a thin napkin. "You can't go staining my clothes before I get to show them off!"

I took the napkin and draped it across my lap.

"Sorry. I'm starving," I said, resting my elbows on the table in another faux pas.

Madison shook her head and turned her attention to the students gathered around a nearby marble fountain. The sunlight reflected off the water, scattering across the pavement in blinding waves of light. Until I'd arrived at FU, I never knew a college campus could be so dramatic. I'd thought most universities seemed sterile and boring. But the FU campus had been built with classic aesthetics in a Southern Gothic style that never aged.

The sidewalks were lined with trees, manicured flower beds surrounded the buildings, the corridors grew thick with ivy, and sculptured water features decorated nearly every corner. The grounds alone were worth paying the hefty tuition fees, especially on days like this. As a new student, I spent a lot of time outside, meandering about the campus or studying under one of these shady trees. But the days of stopping and smelling the roses were few and far between.

I stretched my arms up and over my head, reaching toward the treetop, as I soaked up the warm, filtered sunshine while I could. Autumn was my absolute favorite time of the year. The leaves were falling, and the breeze had a familiar bite to it, which always signaled winter was right around the corner. Before too long, the days would grow short, and I'd hibernate at home in my oversize hoodie and cashmere leggings. I'd slip on my designer leather boots and walk to the coffee shop, wrapped in a scarf the size of a blanket. Nothing felt better than autumn to a basic bitch like me.

I lived for this season when I could turn on Hallmark specials and flip the switch on the common room fireplace for the other BAD basic bitches. We would order caramel apples from the candy shop, stock up on pumpkin butter–scented candles, and pore over this season's fashion trend magazines.

I took a deep breath and exhaled slowly in one long sigh.

"Ahhh. Best time of the year. Crisp, colorful leaves. Hot mugs of cocoa. Flannel pajamas," I said, throwing my head back and sniffing the air again.

"Did you just say, flannel pajamas?" Madison wrinkled her nose.

"Guilty pleasure. Besides, you like scrunchies," I teased.

"Those are back in style. You wouldn't catch me dead in flannel though." She raked her food around with her fork, taking tiny nibbles between her overly plumped lips. She'd had injections yesterday, and though the lipstick covered her bruises, I could tell she'd regretted asking for those extra ccs.

"I live for autumn." I shrugged, scarfing down the rest of my meal

"Not me! Give me a hot summer day and tanned skin on the beach over all this sweater mumbo jumbo, and I'm happy. I think I need to live in a coastal town. I don't want four seasons unless it's the Four Seasons, preferably in Paris. Or Milan. I'm not picky." She set her fork down and touched her lips with her fingertips, wincing. It was a wonder she could flap her jaws so much after her procedure, but Madison never shut up. Even in pain, she kept going.

"Ha!" I scoffed. "Madison Sheffield, not picky." I licked my fork clean and set it in my empty bowl.

"I'm not. That's why I got us Sigmas for the party tonight." She pushed her food away, half-uneaten.

"You got us dates? With Sigmas?" I asked, sucking in my breath.

"You told me to keep your mind off Dominick. This is how we're doing it."

"But Sigmas!" I protested. My voice rose, drawing the attention of everyone near us.

She leaned forward, putting her bony elbows on the table. "Think about it. Sigmas are the most notorious playboys in the history of FU. Their fraternity house is only good for two things—partying and sex. What better way to blow off some steam than to get wild for a night with men who know how to show women a good time?" she said before wincing and touching her lips again.

"Yeah, I guess there's truth to that," I mused, half-excited and half-terrified.

I'd never had the chance to party too wildly, and I wasn't sure I wanted to. I could see myself taking one step into a free-spirited lifestyle and going overboard. These days, it wouldn't take much for me to hop on the back of some man's motorcycle and not look back.

"So, this Halloween party ... do you think Dominick will be there?" I asked, lowering my voice when I said his name.

"I don't know. But if he is, you won't know. He'll probably be wearing a costume, and so will you. Come on. Let's start getting our shit together, so we can rock this night. Cheri's too damn busy working—again—to come out to play, but so far, I think everyone else will be tagging along!"

I nodded, following her lead.

Even in a costume, I'd know Dominick. That raw animal magnetism he'd mentioned would pull me straight back into his grasp. I'd felt the pull now, just speaking his name aloud. If he showed up at the Halloween party, I was doomed.

The BAD traditional requirement for certain holidays stated every sister needed to match and be coordinated at any given event. That meant, Halloween, Christmas, Valentine's Day, and Easter was a team effort in the wardrobe department. Last Easter, we had stood in a seamless line of pastels, and the year before, we had worn faux fur everything à la the Easter Bunny. But the outlandish requests for Halloween themes were always the most fun.

Of course, as fashion students, we took our costumes very seriously. Last year, we'd graced local Halloween parties as Disney princesses, dressed head to toe in silks and chiffons and drenched in glitter and sequins. But this year, our dear leader, Madison, had chosen a different, edgier route and declared we transform ourselves into villains. Madison, first as always, had claimed the character of Cruella de Vil. Her stark white hair and sharp bone structure guaranteed her the part even if someone was stupid enough to object.

I'd grabbed the Queen of Hearts role because it seemed basic enough with the hint of a bite I needed tonight. I didn't want to walk into the party with horns like Maleficent or figure out how to pull off tentacles like Ursula. I wanted to be cute, covered in hearts, crowned, and cutthroat. I was pretending to be both a queen and a villain after all.

"Ladies! Ladies! Everyone, gather around for photos!" Madison yelled, throwing the coattails of her dalmatian-print jacket behind her. Her long hair was parted straight down the middle with one side her usual white and the other as black as midnight. She'd sworn the black hair spray was supposed to wash out easily, but lucky for her, she could pull the look off even if it stuck. Knowing Madison's talent with trends, the younger girls on campus would begin dyeing half their heads tomorrow.

"I'll take the photos since I'm the party pooper and I can't go!" Cheri hopped down the stairs in an oversize navy boyfriend sweater and knee-high knitted socks. I knew she probably wore leather straps underneath.

I never understood why she'd chosen to be a cam girl. Her parents owned eight vineyards to the north and four on the West Coast.

She was part of the Forks' elite crowd and could buy anything she wanted. But whatever she was doing on her bed in front of her laptop must have been worth it because I hardly ever saw her these days. She had a different virtual sugar daddy every other week.

This last Wednesday, on our weekly girls' night, she'd invited Madison and me to her room, promising us that her cameras were turned off——unless we wanted to join in on some fun. I politely declined, but Madison thought about it for a minute before declaring she wasn't drunk enough.

Cheri showed us a jewelry box stuffed with diamonds, a closet full of brand names I hadn't even known we could buy in Forks, and her virtual bank account——all from her online fans. My jaw dropped, but Madison didn't seem as impressed. She'd had a ridiculous amount of money her entire life. Me, on the other hand, I wasn't even in the same ballpark of those two. I'd crawled into bed that night, contemplating giving up on school and becoming a porn star. But then how would I get use out of my designer outfits when I had to be naked most of the time? I could be practical.

I popped a bottle of rosé bubbly and began filling glasses for the crowd gathered around us.

"All right, everyone, circle around. Hold your champagne up and say cheers on the count of three. We're shooting a video first. Then, head to the staircase. One, two, three!" Madison shouted.

"Cheers!" the girls yelled before erupting into laughter. Already, they'd snuck into the liquor cabinet.

"Girls, girls, girls! Don't drink too much! Remember the rules! Now, shut your fool mouths and get your asses on those stairs before I skin you alive!" Madison bellowed in her best Cruella command. It worked.

The girls fell into silence and scurried up the stairs.

"Phenomenal impression. You should pretend to be a villain more often to get these ladies to listen to you," I said, smirking.

"Who said I'm pretending? I don't pretend. I'm just me in all of my fabulousness." She tossed her hair over her shoulder and marched toward the staircase.

It took twenty minutes to get two passable photos every sister could agree upon, so we could hashtag ourselves all over the internet before heading to the party. By the time we finally squished into the rental limousine, courtesy of Ms. Sheffield, it was near ten p.m. The driver took off as I settled into my seat while Madison went over the rules for the third time. She reminded everyone we were only to pretend to drink. She didn't want to stumble upon any of us facedown and ass up on the kitchen table, offering ourselves for body shots. Everyone agreed—some reluctantly.

I didn't mind the *no drinking at parties* rule. I planned on blowing off steam in other ways. After Madison had told me she'd gotten us dates from Sigma, I'd panicked. But the more I'd thought about it, the idea of fooling around with a man who knew how to handle me was more than tempting.

I lost myself in excited chatter until the limo turned down Greek Row. My heart lurched into my throat as we pulled to a stop in front of the Sigma house.

"We're here. Don't forget the rules. Have a good time. If you run into any trouble, get me right away. Watch your drinks, but better yet, don't drink them! This isn't a game, people. I know you all think this is the funhouse, but it's serious. There's a reason for their bad-boy reputation. Some are downright dangerous." Madison wagged her finger in the air.

A couple of girls in the back giggled.

"I think they got it. Let them live a little. Besides, we're blowing off steam tonight too," I said, leaning into Madison while the girls filed out of the limo.

"Speaking of, there are our dates. Let's go!" She grinned before tilting her head toward two men waving from the porch steps.

I peered out the window, trying to get a good look at who would hopefully manhandle me tonight. Both men stood, rocking back on their heels, with their hands shoved in their high-waisted pants. They wore skintight white belly shirts underneath red suspenders. Even from the street, I could see the sweet ripple of abs. One of the men had a bandana tied around his head, and the other wore a toboggan. They both wore oversize mustaches that wiggled like a cat's tail each time they opened their mouths.

"You set us up with fucking Cheech and Chong?" I paused before hurrying out of the limo behind her.

"Relax. They're hot underneath whatever fluffy shit's pasted on their gorgeous faces. They're twins, so we won't have to fight over them."

"I don't think I'll be fighting over them or their plastered face pubes. You can have both ... at the same time if you want. I'll find a fireman or a sailor or someone who looks like they can rock my world, not take me on a trip with a pocketful of shrooms," I hissed, gathering my petticoat skirt in my fists and sliding out the door with my legs closed to avoid a crotch shot.

"Hailey!" Madison cackled. "I promise they'll show us a good time. You'll see later when you peel all the hair off his face. Now, come on. We need fun. These two are as fun as it gets. Trust me. I know that more than anyone." She stepped out of the limo and straightened her fur coat before hooking her elbow with mine.

"Whatever. Let's just get on with it," I muttered.

We slipped through the lively crowd and toward the two goobers dancing on the porch. Dozens of students congregated in the front yard, sipping warm beer out of their red plastic cups. They casually crept toward the house before stalling and chickening out. I couldn't blame them. Everything about Sigma spelled danger. From the rumored basement orgy room to the resident ecstasy dealer, this fraternity was only an excuse for trouble.

"Hey, man. I think I'm tripping. Look! It's fucking Cruella de Vil. You seeing this shit, man?" Cheech smacked Chong on the shoulder with the back of his hand.

Chong stumbled back dramatically.

"That must have been some dope dope, man." Chong rubbed his shoulder before bowing at my feet. "Your Majesty." He cleared his throat.

"Can you two break character for one minute and not freak my friend out?" Madison pulled Chong to his feet and flicked his mustache.

"Sorry. We tend to lose all self-control when we see incredibly beautiful ladies. Especially those dressed as BAD girls." Cheech winked at me.

I studied his face under the porch lights and immediately regretted the instant judgment I'd cast on the twins.

"Villains. We're villains tonight," Madison snapped, jutting out her hip in her signature pose.

"Oh, sorry. Villains! Well, I'm Cheech or Jace, whatever you prefer to call me. This here is my brother from the same mother, Matt, or Chong. Whatever floats your boat." Cheech stuck out his hand.

"Nice to meet you two. I'm Hailey." I shook his hand and looked over at Chong, who towered me.

Even with the ridiculously bushy mustache, Matt had the chiseled bone structure of a god. His dark eyes matched the rugged black hair peeking out from under his bandana. I skimmed over his sharp jawline that led to one of those masculine butt chins. Damn, I loved a good butt chin. Madison was right. Upon closer inspection, these men were fire, and I was done for. Just stick a fork in me—or Chong. Whatever. I was a goner, off in my own fantasy Wonderland already.

"The Queen of Hearts, who stole my heart." Matt reached for my hand and pulled it to his lips. He brushed his scraggly stache against my knuckles, sending goose bumps up my thighs and a wiggle through my hips.

"All right. I think I like you two better when you're Cheech and Chong. None of this chivalrous bullshit. I reached out to you for a reason. My girl and I need a good time. It's been a rough semester." Madison stepped into Jace, sliding one finger down from his collar to his zipper.

"Say no more, man. Follow me." Jace whirled around and pushed the front door open.

"After you." Matt moved aside, letting me pass.

I stepped inside Sigma, and it was like falling down the rabbit hole to the other side of college—the darker, filthier side. I softened, tossing my inhibitions out of the window the further into the house we went, away from curious eyes. We winded our way through a narrow hall and past a door rattling on its hinges. The moans coming from the other side were muffled by the tunes echoing off the walls. I hoped Matt could coax out moans like that from me tonight.

My previous boyfriends hadn't been good enough to make me shout out in ecstasy, but then again, they hadn't tried very hard. Instead of screaming out during sex, I usually came with a dull hum in an *oh, this feels nice* sort of way. But I didn't want to feel nice anymore. I wanted to feel wild, reckless, and nothing like basic.

I caught sight of Jen at the other end of the hallway, dressed in a devil's cape and demon horns. She stood with her back against the wall, talking to a muscular man in a police uniform. His arm was outstretched, his hand beside her, as he leaned in, whispering in her ear.

"What the fuck is she doing here?" I shouted above the music, pulling on Madison's shoulder to get her to stop.

"Probably the same thing we're doing. Having a good time. Just ignore her. At least she isn't with Joel or … the other one." Madison shrugged and continued following behind Jace, disappearing into the crowd.

"You doing okay?" Matt asked.

"Yeah, I'm good. It's just really crowded in here." I tugged at my collar, fanning myself while also giving him a quick flash down my dress—a move I'd learned from Madison. To hell with classy tonight.

His voice grew husky. "Let's find a place to sit and … chat." He reached for my hand, stepping in front of me and leading the way into a large, open room.

I clung to Matt, blindly following him while my eyes adjusted to the dark.

The last time I'd been in the Sigma common room, I'd watched as two drunken girls snorted cocaine off each other's breasts. I recognized them from school. Cheri said they were studying to be nurses. But once their clothes started coming off, Madison and I'd had some serious conversations. That was the night we'd decided on our new house rules. We had to keep in line and not snort lines. Easy enough.

"Have you been here before?" Matt asked. He pressed his hand on my lower back and steered me toward a group of couches.

"Once. A long time ago." I shivered. The touch of his palm sent a warm flush between my legs.

The Sigma boys knew exactly how to make a woman feel good. There was no doubt about that. They were the type of boy toy you slipped under to get over someone else. Madison couldn't have planned a more perfect intervention for me.

"Hey! There you are. I lost you for a second. Let's go get a drink." Madison appeared again, stepping between Matt and me.

"I can grab some drinks. Just go have a seat over there." Matt stuck his butt chin in the direction of a cluster of couches and chairs.

"No. It's okay. We can—" Madison said, but Matt had already turned to leave.

"What is it?" I craned my neck around her, but she stood on her heels, blocking my view.

"It's nothing. Just … let's sit somewhere else, okay?" she spoke quickly.

"Madison, don't lie to me. Please." My breathing quickened.

I hadn't seen her worried before. She never showed emotion, claiming it wrinkled her face and prematurely aged her.

"You told me to help you get over him. This is me helping. You don't want to go over there," she said, squaring her shoulders and standing her ground.

"Yes, I do. I need to see. Show me." I tried to push past her, but she blocked my path.

"No, you don't. Listen to me, Hailey. We need to go somewhere else." She dug her heels into the ground like a bull ready to charge.

"Damn it! Is Diana over there, doing tequila shots?" I pointed in the other direction and made my break as soon as Madison turned her head.

"Wait!" she shouted, scurrying behind me.

On the couch at the back of the room sat Preston and Dominick with three barely dressed women. Two of the women were completely topless, clad in only garter belts and fishnet stockings. They were sucking each other's faces off, leaning across Preston, who sat between them. He'd entangled his hands in their hair, pushing their heads together, as if they were his puppets. All three of them wore matching masquerade masks.

Beside him sat Dominick, dressed in a fedora and a striped business suit. His arm was lazily slung around the other half-naked woman. She draped her long legs over his hips and traced his mouth with her finger. His lips parted in his familiar, dazzling smirk as he followed her eyes with his. He pulled her on his lap in one quick motion, blocking my view of his face. All I could see was his tatted-up forearms slipping down her dress, putting her boobs directly in his face.

A burning sensation shot through my chest, causing me to stumble into Madison, who stood at my back, ready to catch me.

"I told you not to go over there. Come on. We can find somewhere else to sit," she said.

"No." I clenched my jaw. I wanted nothing more than to run away from this place, but I had come here for a reason. And that reason was to get over the man who had clearly forgotten me. "I'm not letting a Moretti stand in my way. I'm going over there to sit and make out with Chong right in front of him."

"Hailey"—Madison grinned—"this isn't like you. It's more like me. Are you sure you want to play this game? Because I can totally play this game. I just know you wanted me to keep him off your mind, and, well, he's practically fucking that chick on the couch over there so …"

"Who is she anyway?" I asked, curling my lip and baring my teeth.

"I can't tell from here. But she sure as fuck isn't the BADass Queen of Hearts. Adjust your crown, and let's go. I'm going to show Preston I'm not his best friend's little sister anymore, and you're going to show that damn Moretti that he's nothing to you."

I lifted my chin and threw my shoulders back, marching right past them and toward Jace, who stood next to a couch directly across from Dominick.

"I thought I'd lost you two! Where's Matt?" Jace asked, pulling off his toboggan and shaking out his disheveled hair. It hung from his head in tattered strands. If he were mine, I'd thread my fingers through it and give it a playful tug.

"To get drinks. Why don't you go help him?" Madison stepped into Jace and ran her palm down his bicep before snapping his suspender against his chest.

"Your wish is my command," he growled before putting his hat back on and disappearing into the crowd behind us.

"You trust they won't roofie us?" I spread my skirt and settled onto the couch, trying and failing to ignore the DIKs in front of me.

"Oh gosh, no. I've known them since I was a kid. They're harmless booty calls. We aren't drinking anyway." She sat down, pulling off her coat and smoothing down her skintight dress.

"Speak for yourself. I need a drink." I forced myself to look away from the girl straddling Dominick's lap.

Madison sighed. "If it loosens you up, fine. But as soon as those boys come back, we're having a good time. Not on trashy display like those thots though. Just follow my lead."

Matt and Jace came back with their hands full.

"We didn't know if you wanted shots, beer, or margaritas, man. So, we got a bit of everything. Enjoy," Matt said, back in character. He set the drinks on the table in front of us, taking a beer for himself.

"Ah, what the hell?" Madison said, tearing her gaze from Preston, who was kissing both women in a tangle of tongues. She grabbed a shot from the table and swallowed it whole before licking her still-swollen lips.

I grabbed a shot and followed suit, gulping it down until my throat burned raw. At least the whiskey burn distracted me from the searing ache in my chest. For a brief moment, I didn't feel anything, except the alcohol.

Perfect.

I grabbed another, throwing it back, and it slid down my throat a little easier.

The twins exchanged grins and sat down beside us.

"All right, man, let's get this party started." Jace pulled a fat joint out from behind his ear and lit it. He smoked a few puffs before handing it over to Madison.

She glanced around to make sure no one was watching before grabbing the joint from his hand and clamping her plump lips around it. She took a drag, held it, and blew a stream of heavy smoke out of the side of her mouth, laughing and waving it away, before handing it over to me.

"Pain management for these new lips." She pushed her lips out, making a kissy face.

"Sure it is. I'll pass. But hand me that drink over there." I nodded toward a cup on the table before giving the joint to Matt.

Madison narrowed her eyes and gave me the cup.

Matt laid his head back on the sofa and put the joint to his lips. He inhaled, lighting the end in a fiery blaze. A piece of burning ash fell off the tip and into his fake mustache, setting it to smoldering. He took another drag off the joint, oblivious to the hot ash kindling above his lip.

"Hey, dude. I think your beard's burning," Jace said in his best Cheech impersonation.

Matt turned his head toward us, laughing. "Nah, man. You're just high. This smoke's coming from my mouth. See?" He inhaled another puff and blew out a stream of smoke. His mustache sparked.

I scrunched my nose at the scent of burning artificial hair.

"No, I think you're really on fire," I said, scooting away from him as half his mustache began to glow brighter.

"Thanks, babe. You're fire too," he answered slowly with half-lidded eyes.

I had a feeling he was high on a lot more than booze and pot.

"No, dude. Fuck, I'm serious." Jace reached over both Madison and me and ripped Matt's mustache off his face. He fanned it in the air, putting it out before tossing it on the table.

It looked like a singed hairpiece, similar to the frizzed extensions I'd mistakenly opted for years ago. I'd looked like I'd stuck my finger in an electrical outlet once I left the salon. I had taken one glance in the mirror and refused to go until the stylist gave me my normal hair back.

Matt tilted his head this way and that, like a dog trying to figure out his situation.

"Ow." He rubbed his hand across his naked lips. "What'd ya do that for?"

His reaction had come about thirty seconds too late.

"You were on fire!" I laughed.

I'd thought he was hot before, but without his fake stache, Matt was downright edible. I didn't care if he was as high as a kite or dumb as a rock. I'd quickly forget Dominick with this man's face smothering mine. I shifted closer to him, rubbing my thigh against his.

"Oh. Fuck. What happened?" His brows scrunched together while he continued rubbing his upper lip.

"Never mind." I shook my head.

Madison puffed from the joint, tilting her head back and blowing smoke rings in the air. I'd never known she could do a trick like that. But from the rumors about her taboo bedroom adventures, whatever tricks she performed with her mouth and tongue didn't surprise me.

"Want to feel them?" she asked Jace.

"Feel what?" He grinned, his eyes shooting straight to her chest.

"My lips. I just got them done." She stubbed the joint out on a coaster and puckered up.

"Yeah, man. I've never felt fake lips before." He reached out to touch them, but she swatted his hands away.

"Not like that. Like this," she purred, pulling Jace by his suspenders straight into her lips.

They entangled themselves together in a rush of raw lust. I blinked, wondering if I was seeing them right or if I was high from everyone's secondhand smoke.

"Well, that escalated quickly." I shifted my gaze from my best friend after I noticed her hand moving up Jace's thigh.

"That looks fun," Matt said, staring at my bottom lip before leaning down and taking it between his teeth.

I gasped before giving in and kissing him back.

"I need more than fun," I whispered into his mouth. "So much more."

"I'm your man. I'm a love machine," he said, circling his arms around me.

He nibbled his way down my neck, shoulder, and arm. I uncrossed my legs and let his hand trail up my inner thigh. His mouth swept over my collarbone and back up to my ear.

"Let's get out of here," he whispered.

I side-eyed Dominick across from me. The woman on his lap arched her back and tilted her head behind her. His eyes flickered up and over her breasts, landing directly on Matt and me. Time stood still—or at least, my reaction felt as slow as Matt. Dominick's usual flashy grin turned deadly in a heartbeat—my thumping heartbeat. I tensed, unable to move or respond to my date. I'd seen the look of fury on Dominick before. He'd worn the same expression when Joel grabbed my arm. If I didn't run, Matt was about to get whacked.

Dominick shifted the half-naked lady off his lap and rose to his feet in a ninja move that would've been comical if I wasn't facing a life-or-death situation. My breath caught in my throat.

"I need to run to the bathroom. Sorry. I'll be right back." I stumbled over his legs and disappeared into the crowd.

I didn't have to look behind me to know Dominick was on my heels. I'd been chased by him before, but this was different. The fury in his eyes had signaled the danger everyone had warned me about several times, but I'd stupidly ignored it.

I clutched my chest, running through hall after hall, twisting and turning until he trapped me in a deserted dead end. I swallowed hard, braced myself, and turned around. I was the Queen of Hearts. I could flip him my middle finger as I shouted, *Off with your head,* and leave if I wanted to. But I didn't want to.

"What're you doing here?" His voice lashed out as he barreled toward me, stopping only inches away.

I could smell her on him. She smelled of cheap knockoff perfume—eau de skank.

"I could ask you the same thing!" I backed up, curling my fists until my fingernails dug into my palms. My breaths rattled in my chest. The image of him and the other woman remained stuck in my head.

He paced back and forth in the hall, catching his breath before speaking again, "This place is dangerous. You shouldn't be here. I'm taking you home. Let's go." He reached out, holding my hand in his.

"Oh, yeah? You talking to me is dangerous too, and yet here you are. Do you think I care anymore? I've been living in a bubble my entire life. I don't want to tonight! I'm allowed to let loose. So, don't fucking touch me." I yanked my arm from his grasp.

He held his hands up and backed away. A shadow crossed the end of the hall, pausing for a moment before disappearing again.

"You're planning on having a wild night with a Sigma then?" he asked. The muscle in his jaw twitched.

"And you're planning on having a wild night with that ratchet girl?" I hissed, folding my arms across my chest.

"I wasn't planning on anything, Hailey." He lowered his voice, glancing over his shoulder.

"Certainly not with me," I said.

"What's that mean?" He took a step closer.

The heat radiating from his body warmed my cold shoulder. I bit my lip, refusing to melt into a puddle of tears right in front of him.

"Nothing. Never mind." I blinked, looking up at the ceiling to keep my eyes from welling over.

"I thought this was done. We were done. That's what you said, right? What do you want me to say? We were on a break!" He tilted his head, studying my face.

"Don't even try to be funny right now, Dominick," I spit his name out like venom. "Besides, that *Friends* show is overrated. Just like you and the rest of the Morettis." I tried to shove my way past him. I wanted to go home.

"Wait," he commanded, putting his arm up and barring me from leaving. "Fine. I thought you'd like funny, considering you were just over there, getting tag-teamed by Cheech and Chong. But I guess you must not be looking for funny tonight. You must want something else. Pretending again, are you? How come every time I see you, you're in costume anyway?"

"It's a fucking costume party. Just like the one you invited me to at the bar. Maybe you need a damn disguise because you don't have the balls to be seen with me."

Adrenaline coursed through my veins, and I broke out into a nervous sweat. Every part of my body tingled—from my brain down to my big toe. I curled it in my shoe, making sure I wasn't imagining things. I was probably still buzzed from marinating in weed smoke back in the common room.

He clamped his mouth shut, breathing hard through his nose and staring right through me. With each step he took toward me, I took a step back until my heels hit the wall.

"And, yes," I stammered, "I was looking for some fun. Lots and lots of fun. Just like the fun you were having with whoever naked chick was. Except more funner." I pointed my finger in his face. "Lots more funner! And nakeder and wilder!" I threw my hands in the air, still seething with a mixture of hurt, pain, anxiety, and whatever the hell my big toe was doing.

He bared his perfect teeth, pushing my hand out of his face. His hands clasped around my middle, spinning me around and forcing me against the wall. He grabbed my wrists and pinned them behind my back, twisting them in his grip.

"If you wanted me to fuck you, Hailey, why didn't you just say so?" he growled into my ear.

I squirmed in his grasp but didn't fight him off. Instead, I turned my head and locked my eyes on his.

"Then, fucking do it," I dared him.

Eight

DOMINICK

Those four words—*then, fucking do it*—was all I needed to hear to make Hailey Simmons mine.

"Let's go," I said, pulling her toward the door a little rougher than I'd meant to handle her.

In the last few weeks, I'd done nothing but think about the way she'd bared herself behind the shed. Countless nights, I'd lost sleep, mulling over our last conversation. I'd caught a glimpse of the void in her eyes that day, and I'd never understood anything more. She possessed me, every bit of me, and now, it was my turn to possess her.

"Wait! Someone's going to see us! I need to text Madison. What about Preston?" She curled her palm in mine, struggling to keep up with my pace.

"I don't give a fuck." I jerked my head around the hall, daring anyone to question us.

The sight of her with that Chong asswad had activated my beast mode—or as my family liked to call it, the legendary Italian temper. Nothing could stop me from getting my way when my anger flared. I wanted what I wanted. And what I wanted was Hailey's legs spread in front of me while I tore her pussy up. I'd give her what she was begging for while taking what I needed.

I led us through the crowd and into my Jeep before she spoke another word.

"Take me home," she said, squirming in her seat. "No one's there."

"I'm on it." I stomped my foot on the gas pedal.

She lifted her dress, exposing dainty black lace panties, and I reached over, sliding my hand between her damp thighs My cock strained against my pants as I rushed us toward her house. I needed those thighs wrapped around my neck, squeezing me with each flick of my tongue over her velvet pussy.

I pulled her panties to the side and pushed my finger up her wet slit. She moaned, grabbing my hand and shoving it harder against her. I slipped a finger inside and then another as she bucked against my knuckles. I spread my palm and let her ride my hand as I maneuvered the car around and finally pulled in front of her sorority house.

She pushed my hand away and leaned over the seat, unzipping my pants and diving straight into my cock. She licked the tip of my dick, working her way down the shaft and cupping my balls before wrapping her lips around me entirely. My hips rose in the seat as I gripped the steering wheel with one hand and tangled her bubblegum-pink hair in the other. I pushed her head further down, testing to see how much of me she could handle.

She moaned and gagged, taking me whole before coming up for air. The streetlights reflected off her damp skin, highlighting the pulse beating in the hollow of her neck. I needed to put my mouth there to feel those ripples under my tongue.

"Ready?" She swept her thumb over the corner of her mouth, wiping the wetness from her bottom lip.

A charge of excitement shot through me as I imagined her head tilted back and my cum dribbling down her chin.

"Show me to your room," I said, tucking myself back into my pants and hopping out of the Jeep.

She rushed to my side, tugging my arm toward the side entrance.

"Only Cheri should be here, but she's upstairs in her room, working. I'm on the opposite end of the hall, so I doubt she'll know anyone's home. Come on!"

I followed as she led us through a massive kitchen that looked as if it had never been used, a marble-tiled breezeway with an oversize chandelier, and up a winding staircase that widened into a lofty study.

"I'm in the west wing." She nodded toward the hall on the left, hesitating.

I didn't have time to wait. My dick was still throbbing in my pants with an urgent need to fill her up. I put a hand to the curve of her lower back and pushed her toward her room.

"We're he—" she started, stopping in front of her door.

I clasped my hand around her jaw and brought her lips to mine, muffling her voice with my mouth. I stepped into her room, walking her backward through the door before kicking it shut with my foot. She'd left the blinds open, letting enough light in to wash over us both.

I'd been dreaming about this moment since I first laid eyes on her after the prank she pulled in the DIK house. She had practically been begging for punishment after that. I knew enough about women to know what she wanted even if she was too stubborn to admit it.

I kept pushing her back until we bumped against a mirror and dresser. I swung her around, bending her over the top and forcing her to face our reflection.

"Is this what you wanted, Hailey?" I whispered, grabbing a fistful of her hair and pulling her head up to watch what I was about to do.

Her mouth opened slightly before she quickly shut it tight and stared back at me, lifting her chin.

"Ah, still pretending. What's wrong? Can't submit to a Moretti? I know what you want, and I got what you need," I said, pressing my erection against her ass.

I unzipped the back of her dress and let it fall to the floor while she fumbled with her hands, reaching around and unhooking her bra. She shimmied out of it, throwing it to the side.

"Good girl," I said, sliding my palm up and down her bare back.

Her flesh prickled under my fingertips. I circled both hands on her hips before gathering her panties in my fists and pulling, ripping them apart while I watched her expression in the mirror.

She swayed and let out a shaky breath. Her eyes locked on mine.

I slapped my hand hard against her ass, leaving a blushing red mark that shone, even in this dim light.

"Fuck," she moaned. A shudder passed through her as she reached out, steadying herself against the dresser.

I pulled her back into me, spun her around, and lifted her ass on top of the dresser.

"That's my girl. Going to moan for me like that again?" I asked, grabbing her breasts in my hands and sucking her nipple between my teeth and tongue.

She lowered her thick black lashes and whimpered, bracing herself against the mirror.

"I said"—I stood back up, meeting her gaze while sliding my fingertips up and down her pussy—"are you going to moan for me like that again?" I shoved two fingers inside of her, curling them until I hammered against her G-spot.

"Oh fuck. Yes." She squirmed against my hand.

I held her against the mirror with my other arm as I leaned down and teased her lips apart with my tongue. She tasted every bit as sweet as I'd imagined. I licked and finger-fucked her pussy, lapping her up until she dripped down my chin and I knew she was ready. I threw her legs over my shoulders and slipped my hands underneath her ass, carrying her over to the bed while she was still in my mouth. She tensed her thighs, squeezing them around my cheeks and holding on tight.

I gave her clit a gentle nibble before tossing her on the bed. She reached toward a nightstand and pulled out a condom, setting it in front of me. My eyes roamed over her naked figure while she watched me undress. A sheen of sweat glistened over her breasts, illuminating her hardened nipples. Her hips tapered into long, straight legs that she held together tight at the knees, swaying them back and forth, teasing me.

I tore the condom open with my teeth, rolled it on, and stood before her, completely naked, as I drank her in before devouring her. She dug her heels into the bed and pushed herself up toward the headboard. Climbing on top, I towered over her body, grasping her knees and easing them apart. I took my cock in my hand, carefully studying her face, and slid right into her.

We breathed a sigh of relief as soon as I entered the slick heat between her legs. Her eyes widened as I thrust into her hard, again and again. I gripped the headboard and dived deep. She threw her arms to the sides, grasping the sheets in her fists and crying out. A hint of pain flashed in her eyes, but she shook her head at me.

"Don't stop," she breathed out.

I buried myself into her, pushing down and up until I rubbed against her clit with each thrust. She wrapped her legs around me and grabbed my hips, shoving me in harder.

"More," she pleaded, breathless.

A restless, savage lust overtook me, narrowing my vision and focus into one thing—taking what I wanted. I gripped the back headboard harder, slamming against her with all my force. She winced, but took me like a champ, and nodded for me to keep going. I picked up my pace as she bucked against my hips, matching my rhythm.

Her body began to vibrate. She reached out, pulling me down and clutching me to her. Her heartbeat throbbed against my chest while her legs began to shake behind me. She clawed her fingernails into my back and cried out over my shoulder. I collapsed, breathing in her candy-sweet scent, and spilled out inside of her. Her pussy clenched, spasming around my cock and drawing every last drop out of me until I had nothing left to give.

I brushed the pink curls from her face, gently kissing her forehead, the tip of her nose, her brow, her cheeks, and her lips while she slowed her breathing. I lifted myself and rolled to my back, staring at the ceiling. The whirl of the fan hummed in the comfortable silence.

"The last thing I want to do is get out of this bed and away from you. But can you tell me where the bathroom is, so I can clean up?" I asked, propping myself up on my elbows.

"Directly across the hall. Here, take this!" she said, jumping out of bed and grabbing a feathered black robe from the back of the door. She swayed her taut figure back over to me and handed me the robe.

"Are you serious? You want me to wear this? I'd rather just get back into my mob costume or go naked!" I said.

"No one's going to see you! Besides, it's Bianca James! Have you ever worn her brand? It's like slipping on butter. I don't know how she gets her fabrics so smooth!"

"Bianca James, eh?" I hopped out of bed and grabbed the robe, holding it between my thumb and index finger.

"Yes, Bianca James. Like the panties you ripped. It's a line of lingerie for both men and women. You'll have to pick up a pair of her boxer briefs. I'd love to see you strut around in those." She sighed before crawling back between the sheets. "You tried to give me your jacket once, and I was too stubborn. Just wear the robe! You're only walking ten feet and back."

"Fine! I'll show you just how tough I am for this little incident not to threaten my masculinity." I threw the robe over my shoulders and melted. The material draped across my skin like a smooth blanket of marshmallows.

"See?" She laughed. "Your face is priceless."

"It's magic." I held my arm out in front of me, inspecting the sleeve "Hmm. I've never been into fashion, but this I could get used to. It's like I'm wrapped in a cocoon made of fluffy clouds. Bonus: it smells like you." I pulled the collar to my nose and took a deep breath. "Your scent drives me wild, you know."

"You drive me wild," she said, smiling.

"One second. I'm going to sashay this robe to the bathroom. Be right back!" I tiptoed out of the room, swirling the robe behind me. After the way I'd wrecked her in bed, there was no question about my masculinity.

I flipped the light switch on in the bathroom and cleaned myself up, disposing of the evidence that I'd just nasty-sexed the one and only woman who was off-limits. There wasn't any turning back now. What was done was done, and hot damn, it was more than I could have ever imagined. Everything about her—from her soft little moans to the way she had clung to me when she orgasmed—all felt so raw and so real, no pretending.

I turned my back to the mirror and peered over my shoulder, lowering my robe and grinning at the claw marks trailing down my shoulders. A battle scar like that was the best fashion accessory. She'd left her label on me, and I hoped she'd do it again. I switched the light back off and made my way back to her bed, sliding in next to her. She was sitting against the headboard, typing into her phone. The blue screen illuminated her beaming face.

"I had to text Madison and tell her I'd made it home. I told her I wasn't feeling well. We're all good on my front as long as no one saw us leave the party together," she said, setting her phone down and snuggling into my chest, entangling her legs with mine.

I threw my arm around her, holding her close. "We'll be fine. Besides, I doubt anyone would fuck with my family. Snitches get stitches after all. Bada bing bada boom." I finger-gunned the ceiling.

"Off with their heads!" She slid her finger across her neck and made a screech.

"The Queen of Hearts in bed with a mob boss. Somehow, this doesn't sound odd at all. Now J. Rab and the Goblin King might have been more my style, but I'm digging being in bed with you under any disguise." I glanced down at her.

"I think I like Dominick Moretti best." She met my eyes.

"Do you?" I asked. I couldn't hide my smile if I tried. It was one of those goofy grins that painfully stretched across my cheeks, from ear to ear.

"Obviously. I can't keep my hands off of you." She traced her nails along my pecs and abs before bringing them to my jawline, like she was sketching my figure in her mind. "You have such an amazing body, and what you did to me just then was exactly what I'd needed. I hadn't even known it could ever be that good."

"And you … you're like heaven, Hailey Simmons."

"Ha. Hardly. Ever since you came into my life, I've been questioning everything. I thought I was happy, but I think I've just been running through the motions because it's all I've ever known. Does that make sense? I do what I'm supposed to do." She drummed her fingers over the tattoos on my forearm. "I mean, I want to do fashion stuff, but I've never ventured into much else. I've been in the Forks bubble my entire life. I don't feel like I'm accomplishing anything meaningful. I've had everything handed to me, and I was okay with that until you showed up. Now, I'm not so sure. I never put the void into words. But I think that's exactly what I've been experiencing lately."

"There's absolutely nothing wrong with being wealthy and working to keep yourself in the lifestyle you want. I hope I didn't give you that impression. The only issue I have for me is the drama surrounding my family's finances, particularly when it comes to your family. I see what money's done to my dad, and I don't want to go down the same road. Maybe some people can handle it and live a good life. But in my circle, all I've ever known is the high level of bullshit entangled with the lifestyle. I'd rather run away and start anew, like a normal college kid." I brushed my fingertips over her shoulder, smoothing the goose bumps from her flesh.

"You'd give it all up?" she asked.

"In a heartbeat. I know it wouldn't be easy. Losing money terrifies me. But I'd like to think I'm smart enough to learn how to live on my own. I don't need to eat on pottery imported from Italy or lounge by a pool carved of stone. I've done all that, and it's nice, but it's not me. I'd rather travel and see the world, watch how other people live. Save some animals," I said.

"Travel! Yes! I haven't gotten to travel much in the last few years. Our family used to take trips every summer, but as I grew older, they became less frequent." She shivered.

The post-sex flush faded from our bodies.

"Where was your favorite place? If you could go anywhere, where would it be?"

I shifted the covers over her shoulder and pulled her into me tighter, warming her body with mine. She curled into me.

"I think Yellowstone. I love the mountains, the rivers, the open ranges. Seeing all the wildlife was amazing. But most of all, it was the only time I can remember my family being happy. I can't even remember my dad working then. Maybe he couldn't because there wasn't any signal in the park, but no matter, he was a different man. I loved that place."

"Ah, I love it out there too! We went once long ago and hiked the Tetons. We were told if we saw a moose, we'd have good luck. I spent the whole damn trip looking for a moose. We never saw anything, except a huge pile of bear shit, but it was still pretty cool! That's the kind of lifestyle I'd prefer. Not all this." I motioned around her room. "No offense."

"So, wait. You'd prefer bear shit to my chandelier and silk curtains?" she scoffed.

"Actually, yeah. Bear shit coupled with the majestic mountains, the scent of budding wildflowers on a warm spring day, the roar of waterfalls at the end of the trails, the sunset over the mountain peaks. Yep."

"Well, all this"—she waved her hand in the air—"isn't just me. Madison's mom built it, and you know she's extravagant. Our house is a constant project for interior design students. It's a lot of work, keeping the home modern and on trend. So, it's not all fancy-schmancy pants just because. It's a work of art and a learning experience. I just so happen to get the benefit of living here and enjoying it."

"But you don't think you'd be happy without these material things?" I asked, raking my fingers through her hair.

"I don't know. I've never tried it. Do I get to keep my designer handbags? Because I do love them. And my shoes. And my Bianca James undies, which I'll now have to buy more of. Thanks, Dom." She laughed. "Oh, and my robe. And mimosas. Fuck. I'm not good at this, am I?"

"Come here, you." I grabbed her, rolling her on top of me until we were face-to-face. "You'd survive without Bianca James because you'd just make your own label—Hailey Simmons. It would be ten times more incredible and feel soft, like melted butter against your ass cheeks."

She threw her head back and laughed, displaying a pink tongue that I longed to have back in my mouth.

"Like butter, eh? That sounds like it would feel so good." She cupped her hand to my chin, running her thumb across my cheek and softening me little by little. "But do you know what I want to feel?"

"No. Tell me. What do you want to feel?" My cock stirred again.

This woman had a hold on me like I'd never felt before. It was both exciting and terrifying.

"Something. Anything," she muttered into my mouth, slipping her tongue between my lips.

I circled my arms behind her, flipping her onto her back. And then I made love to her for the rest of the night.

By the time we were finished in bed, we both realized it was dawn, and my Jeep was still parked in front of the BAD house. I vaguely remembered hearing the girls come in at one point during the night. But Hailey and I'd lost ourselves in our sexcapades, paying little attention to anything but each other. We explored for hours until our bodies were as spent as our minds. Between each session, we'd slowed down and drifted into dreamy pillow talk before ramping back up again in a fit of savage lust. I needed her, and by the way she'd handled me, I knew she needed me too.

"I'll sneak out the side door. They can't be up at this hour. Don't worry, cupcake." I kissed her forehead, brushing her hair from her eyes.

"You never gave me your number, you know," she said, propping up on her elbow and watching me wiggle back into my costume. Her gaze raked over my body like hot coals, and if it wasn't dawn, I'd jump back into her bed.

"Oh. You want to ring me for another booty call?" I winked before pulling out my phone.

"Much more than that. We can be discreet. I'm able to keep a secret. Are you?"

"For you, anything," I said.

She told me her number, and I punched it into my phone and texted her mine. I quickly kissed her good-bye and rushed to the door, powered by adrenaline. I hadn't snuck out of someone's house in the history of ever. I knew sneaking into my house wouldn't be an issue. The brothers wouldn't have a clue where I'd slept—or not slept. But sneaking out of BAD was terrible, especially as a Moretti.

I tiptoed down the stairs and rounded a corner, trying to remember how to get out. Luckily, the downstairs was empty, and my path to the getaway car seemed ridiculously easy. Almost too easy. I knew things had been too good to be true as soon as I made it to my Jeep and Jen Hathaway jogged by.

"Dom?" she asked, eyeing me up and down. Her tight little shorts clung to her sweaty hourglass figure.

"Oh. Hi, Jen!" I said a little too animated for this early in the morning.

"What are you—did you … sleep at the BAD house?" She curled her nose and flinched.

"You left this!" Madison called, running out of the front door with a scarf in her hand. It was blue and bedazzled in sequins. "Wait, Dominick! Don't forget your scarf!"

She came up to me and planted a kiss on my cheek, handing me the scarf. My mouth opened and closed like a fish out of water.

"Hey, Jen." Madison smiled, putting her arm around my back and pulling me to her.

"Hey, Madison. I was just saying hi to Dominick. We go way back. I had no idea you two …" Her eyes shifted back and forth between Madison and me.

"This here's my man." Madison smacked my ass hard. "Well, one of them anyway."

"Cool. Okay. See you around." Jen backed away before turning and jogging further down the road.

When she finally disappeared, I found my voice. "Ugh. Thanks. But you couldn't have found a manlier scarf than this? What's with you BAD women trying to make us men wear your clothes?" I handed the scarf back to her, noting her bloodshot eyes for the first time.

"I don't know what kink you're talking about, but it'd better be one of Hailey's!" she huffed, folding her arms across her chest.

She was wearing mismatched pajamas, a messy bun, and last night's makeup. I wasn't the only one who'd had a good time.

"Of course it's Hailey's kink! Wait. That's not her kink. Never mind. I was with Hailey."

"I hope so. Do you have any idea what it would do to her if she found you fucking around with another sister?"

"No. Why? She's talked to you about me? What did she say?" I couldn't hold my grin back.

"What does it matter what she said? I'm sure, now, you know how she feels about you. And ever since you came around, she's been distant with me! Her best friend! I don't know what you're doing, Moretti, but you'd better keep her safe. I know you and people like you. I'm one of them. She's a good person, and she deserves the best." She thrust her stabby, pointed fingernail in my face.

"You don't know me if you think I'm anything like my parents. Ask Hailey. I don't even care to run with the same crowds you all do. I'd prefer to keep a low profile and live a much simpler life," I said.

She gasped, as if I'd spoken blasphemy. "That's insane. Who wants to give up fame and fortune? Does Hailey know? Because you know she has big plans for her future, and it requires fame and fortune—and not having it destroyed by her worst enemy conning her into bed."

"Is that what you think?" I asked, searching her eyes for a truth about Hailey that I hadn't picked up on.

"No," she sighed. "I know you're not conning her. She's got the infatuation bug. It's just dangerous, you know. I'm trying to protect my friend. Obviously! I just saved both of you from that witch, Jen. How do you know her anyway?"

"I dated her just a few times a while back. She became way too clingy though, and I felt like something was off with her. I'm not sure what, but my parents felt it too. They pretty much banned me from her, like they're doing with Hailey. But I can be discreet until Hailey and I figure it out. Us out, I mean." I scratched my head and glanced back down the street, making sure Jen wouldn't pop up again.

"If your idea of discreet is parking your Jeep outside of our sorority house all night, then you lose. You can do better. I don't want to see my friend get hurt. I believe you if you say you aren't like the rest of us. I don't get it, but to each his own. It takes stomping on some heads to get to the top. You don't have to stomp on any. You're already there. Like me. Not sure why you'd stumble over them on your descent, but okay." She rolled her eyes.

"Damn, you make it sound terrible. I'm not trending downward—or however you put it. I'm just not into the same crowds as you and Hailey, and I think she realizes she isn't either." I snapped my eyes back to her. I could play tough too.

"Don't try to change my best friend, Moretti." Madison's gaze shifted away from me as she tried to hide that she knew what I meant.

"I'm not. But maybe you should step back and see for yourself. I don't think Hailey's as happy as she's pretending to be. I'm not influencing her in any way. I think I'm just the first person she's felt comfortable with to be herself, think for herself, and open up."

"What the hell? You don't think her best friend—me— is her number one go-to with life problems?" she asked.

"I didn't say that! We've never spoken about your relationship. We've barely had time to speak much about anything with all the damn hiding we have to do. I don't want to see her hurt either," I said.

"Then, don't get caught. I ran out here to save your ass, hungover as fuck and looking like I'd been ridden hard and hung out to dry. I had! So, this shit right here is the last thing I wanted to do. Figure it out. Hide it better. If her family finds out, she's done for." She took a deep breath and sighed.

"They won't. Not from her or me anyway." I set my jaw and shot her my best *I mean business* look.

"Good. Snitches get stitches," she said, turning to go and blowing me a kiss that was much more *fuck you* than sweet.

I swallowed hard.

If anyone knew about snitches and stitches, it was me, the son of a mob boss.

Nine

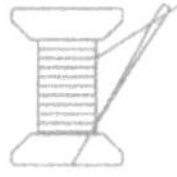

HAILEY

I sighed, stretching my arms over my head and arching my back. I'd only slept three hours, but excitement and adrenaline had kept me too restless to stay in bed. Besides, it was Sunday, which meant mimosas and French pastries on the patio. I figured I'd burned enough calories last night to indulge a little. I hadn't even heard the girls come in last night. No doubt they'd still be asleep if they'd stayed here. I could sneak downstairs and rid myself of this anxious energy before anyone woke to ask me where I'd disappeared to last night.

I reached out, pulling a pillow to my face, breathing it in. Dominick's soapy scent still lingered in my bed.

"Ah! Sweet bliss!" I giggled, clutching it to my chest.

Joel had never made me feel this way. The only scent he'd left lingering was a funky skunk pot smell or body odor from skipping a shower in favor of playing his games.

"Ugh." I gagged, struck with dumbfounded disbelief that I'd stayed so long in a dead relationship when I could have been humping wild men who left me feeling like I could conquer the world—or at least the day.

I winced, rising to my feet. My body ached like I'd run a marathon, climbed a mountain, and swum the sea. Even Madison's workouts never left me this worn out.

"Damn," I whimpered, slipping into my robe.

I hobbled, bowlegged, down the stairs toward the patio. The house was as quiet as it'd ever been and, thankfully, not a single sister was in sight.

I pushed the patio door open, mentally thumbing through all of the positive life changes I'd made on a whim. Dopamine still pumped through my veins, giving me a high and confidence I'd never felt before. I wanted to hike in the woods, take up art and paint landscapes, become a vegan, and find world peace. But I knew my limits. I would drink my mimosa and do some online shopping for more Bianca James first.

"Ahem!" Madison cleared her throat.

I nearly jumped out of my skin at the sight of my poor friend. She looked like death, like she'd crawled out of a grave and then died some more. Her mascara was smeared down her cheeks, and her luscious locks hung, tangled in knots, framing a washed-out face.

"What're you doing up so early? Are you okay? You don't look so good." I poured a mimosa and carried it to the table, setting it beside her empty glass. I snapped a picture, posted it on social media, and hashtagged *brunch vibes.*

"This is the look of someone who had a good time last night. And by the smile on your face and the smile on Dominick Moretti's face this morning, I'd say, you two also had a good time." She swirled her glass and took a sip.

"You saw him this morning?" I sucked in my breath.

"Why didn't you tell me? I thought you told me everything." She took another sip, peering at me over the rim of her champagne flute.

"I do. It was a spur-of-the-moment thing last night. He'd seen me with Matt and gotten jealous, just like you had predicted. One thing led to the other, and we ended up coming back here and having the most incredible night I'd ever had."

I set my jaw and braced myself for the verbal assault she'd surely give me. But instead, she smiled. Whoever had bedded Madison last night must have let her demons out.

"I've been sitting here since he left, trying to figure out the situation. At first, I was hurt. I thought maybe I didn't know you as well as I'd thought. Maybe you'd lied to me because you didn't trust me. Maybe we aren't anything at all alike. But then I realized this isn't about me. You're sneaking around, doing some scandalous shit, and living your best life, and then I became proud. But if I'm going to be an honest bitch, I'll say, I'm worried for you and worried it will change things for me."

I started to object, but she stopped me.

"You know how selfish I am! I see the spark in your eye when you talk about him and the far-off, distant look you have these days. Hell, we don't even talk fashion anymore!" She rubbed the palms of her hands into her eyes and blinked.

"Maybe I'm growing up. I know everyone says people can't really change. But they do. I feel ... different. I don't think it's only Dominick. I think my family and the way they reacted to him and me turned me off too. I've always been told how to act, what to do, what to like. I've not had the chance to think for myself. Maybe I'm not who I think I am. I'm just questioning a lot. But isn't that what happens when people hit college? We meet others from all walks of life, and suddenly, our little bubble we grew up in is popped as we learn what else and who else is out there. Does that make sense?"

"No. I like my bubble. And I can't wrap my head around why you don't." She leaned back in her chair and crossed her arms.

"I didn't say I don't. I just see the light, I guess. Or the truth. Or I wish I could see the truth. But then again, maybe

I don't want to know." I sighed, eyeing the pile of pastries on the plate in front of her. "Ugh! I don't know anymore."

"Just because I don't understand what you're going through doesn't mean I don't support you. I miss my friend. I want you to be able to communicate everything to me. You know I have your back. You and Dom's secret is safe with me. But you'll need a plan to keep it discreet. Jen saw him leaving this morning, and I had to pretend he was with me."

I rubbed my tightening chest and gulped my cocktail before I was able to speak again.

"What was she doing here?" I asked.

"She was jogging by. Caught him while he was leaving. Don't worry. I took care of it. He said he did date her, by the way, but she skeeved him out too. Apparently, you aren't the only one his parents hate." She reached for a Danish, tearing bits and pieces off and popping them in her mouth.

"That's all he said about her? I wonder why they hate her. Jeez, I'm guessing no one will be good enough for their precious son. His mom's probably *that* mom." I rolled my eyes.

"He didn't say anything else. But I'm sure his family has their eyes on him. I'll try to do some digging, too, and figure things out. Maybe there's an easy way out of this for both of you if you want to go down this dangerous road with him. I have mixed feelings about this. On the one hand, I think this is a dumb idea, but on the other, I'm proud as fuck that you're breaking out of your basic little shell," she said.

"Aw, how sweet. My best friend admits she wants the best for me even though I can tell she still wants me for herself." I laughed, tearing off half of a croissant and picking at it.

"I do." She sniffled. "But I'll survive. Plus, I love this shit. I'm kind of excited to be a part of this forbidden romance. You know how good I am with drama." An evil grin spread across her face.

"I'm just glad you're on my side. I'd hate to be up against you. How about we head to the studio in a bit and go over the fashion show? We need to make sure everything's in order and perfect. It's only two weeks away. Besides, I miss studio time with you too."

"Really?" Her bloodshot eyes widened. "Let me down some coffee and take a quick shower. I feel like I've been run over by a train, which I was. Kind of glad you left me with the twins last night." She pushed herself up from the table.

"You didn't!" I gasped, nearly knocking over my drink.

"I did!" she squealed, hobbling toward the door with the same post-sex hobble I'd had this morning.

"Somehow, that doesn't surprise me," I said.

"Touché!" she called behind her before disappearing into the house.

I zoned out to the constant, low humming of the sewing machines. It was only midweek, but I was already exhausted. With the fashion show coming up soon and my new, secret affair with Dominick, life had become busier than ever.

I wanted to make a unique piece for Madison for the event, and finding time to work on it without her knowledge had been tough. If she wasn't in the design studio, she was in the common room. And if she wasn't in the common room, she was with me and the girls, shopping. Last week, we'd scoured eighteen different stores in search of the perfect accessories for gift bags. But true to our nature, we'd treated ourselves and all ended up with a lot more than gift bags. That was when I'd had the idea to gift something special to Madison.

She worked so hard on her brand, the sorority, the fashion show, herself. And lately, I'd been so lost in my head with Dominick and figuring out life that I had been a shit friend.

She'd once claimed a tiger was her spirit animal. Hell, she'd had a huge one tattooed on her arm three years ago when we first started in the sorority. She called herself a tigress, and she wasn't going to let anyone step in her way. And my best friend never faltered in her oath. She rocked her way through the fashion academy like she had been born for the opportunity.

I rocked along beside her, but I hadn't been born for this. I loved design and fashion. But I wasn't nearly as talented as Madison. She deserved to have her brand plastered on an ad in Times Square, and I hoped I could help her get there one day.

"Hey. Think you can fix this tear in my jacket?" Dominick came up behind me, jolting me out of my creative trance. "I was told to come here. I can pay."

I looked around the studio at the other students working away on their projects, but no one paid us any attention. We were all under strict orders from Madison to get the showpieces finished.

"Um, I guess." I lowered my voice.

He'd only spoken a few words, and my heart took off in a race to beat next to his again. I fidgeted in my seat, holding back the urge to throw myself in his arms.

"Sorry for barging in like this. I couldn't help it. I needed to see you." His mouth twisted in a mischievous grin.

"Good. I needed to see your face too." I smiled back at him.

He tilted his head and observed my work in progress.

"Wow! Is that a tiger?" he asked.

"Yeah. It's for Madison. It's going on the inside of a jacket. Kind of a reminder. See this piece right here? I'm going to dye it to match her hair. Then, I'll patch it to this." I held up a bigger swatch of fabric. "It looks like a lot of jumbled mess now, but when it comes together, it will be a super-sexy jacket that I hope she'll love." I stood up from my chair and set my materials aside.

"You're pretty talented," he said, leaning down and inspecting the stitching.

I flushed. I'd never had a man interested in my work before.

"How do I keep running into you?" a woman's voice called from behind us.

We both turned around to catch Jen sneering in the doorway. My heart bottomed out into the pit of my stomach. She lifted her nose in the air, forced a smile, and came our way. Her heels stomped against the tiled floor, echoing like gunshots with each step she took.

Boom. Boom. Boom. Dead.

"I never thought I'd see you two standing side by side. A Moretti and a Simmons. Tsk, tsk. Sounds like trouble." Her tone stabbed like an icicle to the gut.

"I'm sewing his jacket," I said, straightening my back to my full height. I stood a few inches taller than her at least. If she wanted to talk to me, she would need to look up.

"Yep. She just finished and did an excellent job. Thanks, Hailey. I'll let Madison know you were a big help since she's too busy." Dominick turned to go without so much as a glance over his shoulder.

"Hmm. Madison and Dominick. Weird. He sure was standing close to you. I'd heard rumors about Madison and her partners. Someone likes to swap. I'd be careful with Moretti though. He's such a bad boy. They're tempting, aren't they? The most dangerous ones." She twirled her hair around her finger and sighed.

I wanted to slap her across her high cheekbone for the comment about my best friend. But instead, I chose the best response I could give a fake bitch like her. True to my avoidant nature, I didn't respond at all. I gathered my things in my arms and walked away, leaving her behind in a cloud of my signature scent, Chanel No. 5—eau de fuck you.

I marched out of the studio and down the hall before I slowed, noticing his familiar gait echoing behind me.

"Keep going," he whispered loud enough for me to hear. "To the right."

I cut a sharp right and waited, letting him pass. He led us down another hallway and into a janitorial closet. I followed him inside, shutting the door behind me. The scent of cleaning supplies instantly gave me a buzz.

"That was close! You can't just come visit me like that! She's probably the worst snitch in the world, and now, she knows something's up," I said before Dominick crushed his mouth into mine.

He took my bag from my hand, setting it aside on a shelf next to a bleach bottle. I almost objected to my designer bag being so close to danger, but the way his lips trailed down my collar shut me up real quick. I stifled a moan as he knelt before me. He lifted one of my legs and placed it on a lower shelf before sticking his head under my skirt and pulling my panties to the side. I leaned back into the wall, reaching over to steady my sways as he flicked his tongue in feathery strokes across my clit.

I closed my eyes and threw back my head while he hastily spread me with his hands. My hips jerked against his face. I threaded my hand through his hair, tugging it between my fingers and muffling his mouth into me. I bit my lip in an attempt to stop from crying out when he pushed his fingers inside of me. His breaths became heavy and quick, burning hot between my legs. I pulled his hair and fucked his face until I felt myself going over the edge. The release he'd built up inside of me flooded out in a rush of slippery waves. I bucked hard against his jaw.

He lapped me up over and over again until I stopped spasming around his fingers. He dragged his mouth from my pussy, kissing my wet thighs before lowering my skirt and standing up to face me.

"I wasn't expecting that," I said, breathless and momentarily lost in the situation.

I caught a glint of the wet sheen I'd left across his lips. It was the sexiest damn thing I'd ever seen.

"I'm not done with you," he growled, spinning me around and pushing me up against the wall.

I braced myself after I heard the rip of a condom wrapper and the sound of his zipper drop. He knocked my legs apart with his knee and stepped into me, shoving himself inside. His cock slid into me like velvet steel.

I flinched, pushing my cheek into the cold concrete wall. My eyes rolled back with each thrust of his hard cock. He wrapped a forearm around my neck, squeezing my throat into the nook of his elbow while crushing me against the back of the closet His thrusts were explosive, wrecking my pussy until my legs began to shake.

He picked up his pace, slamming into me over and over and stretching me out. I clutched his arm, dug my nails into his bicep, and moaned louder, the harder he fucked me. He covered my mouth with his palm, grunting.

"Fuck," he groaned, tickling the back of my neck with his ragged breaths.

His body shuddered against mine as he buried his face into my back, biting my shoulder and pulsing out inside of me. I felt every twitch of his dick between my swollen lips.

He gently kissed the nape of my neck before pulling out and tucking himself back into his pants. I turned around, stumbling against the wall.

"I'm late for class, but that was worth it. I've been craving you since I left you last. I hate leaving you all the time. I want to take you on a proper date and spoil you a bit." He tapped the end of my nose with his finger and winked.

"I don't need to be spoiled. But fancy cocktails on a patio with your hand on my thigh would be nice. We'd just have to go in disguise again." I smoothed my hair back and wiggled my skirt down.

I couldn't see myself, but after what had just happened to me, I probably looked like I'd just been fucked in a broom closet.

How many basic bitches did that? I huffed on my nails, polishing them against my shoulder.

"I have something we can do without disguise. It's the real reason I came to see you. No, that's a lie. I really wanted you to sit on my face. The second reason I came to see you was because I have to take my aunt Edna to some doctor in Outer Forks. Her caretaker has an early appointment and can't drive her over, but she's meeting me there, so I only need to drop her off. And I was hoping you'd go with me. There's a place called Scarlett Herb nearby. It's the sister restaurant to Bar Thomas. I'll get you those fancy cocktails and a hand on your thigh at no charge."

"I can't meet your family! Are you crazy?" I said.

"It's my aunt Edna. She has Alzheimer's. She won't remember a thing. I promise! It's a way for us to get away without seeming suspicious. We'll have the entire day to ourselves. I can get a hotel room if you want," he said, running the back of his hand down the curve of my cheek.

I shivered back the anxiety that had already begun to bubble in my chest.

"When?" I asked.

"This Saturday. I can pick you up outside Bar Thomas, so no one sees. How about nine in the morning? I should have her settled in the car by then."

"And you're sure she won't tell?"

"She sometimes mistakes me for a talking sheepdog. We'll be fine," he assured me.

"It's a date then. I'll see you Saturday, and I'll take you up on the hotel. As long as you do that thing with your tongue again." I raised my brows and threw him a smirk.

"I'll do more than that." He leaned in, planting a kiss on my forehead. "I've got to run though. I need to, uh"—he paused, pointing to his pants—"clean up."

"Right. And I need to …" I shifted my eyes around the room. I had nothing to do besides finish this project for Madison, which just so happened to double as my final exam. I scratched my head. "Damn, I need a life outside of school."

"I'll be your life outside of school," he whispered, opening the door a crack and peering into the hallway.

"As long as Aunt Edna keeps her mouth shut," I whispered back.

"I'll tell her, snitches get stitches," he said, dragging his finger across his throat before sneaking out of the closet.

I'd spent the rest of the week with my head in the sewing machine or my feet on the treadmill. I'd finally tightened up to pull off Madison's new fitness line and score next year's bikini as a treat to myself for keeping motivated. But motivation wasn't hard to find when my fuck buddy had washboard abs. I couldn't keep my hands or my tongue off of him.

He had what I liked to call a well-defined dick root—the muscle line trailing down his hips to his groin. I'd always wanted to trace a dick root with my lips, my fingertips, my tongue. But meeting up with Dominick proved tricky and often left me frustrated. We spent countless hours texting or talking on the phone when we were between classes. But we'd only had two encounters because sneaking inside my house or his wasn't the easiest thing to do.

He still hadn't told anyone about us—thankfully. And the only person who knew we were messing around from my side was Madison. But she wouldn't tell a soul. She'd even offered to drop me off at Bar Thomas this morning, so my car could remain at home and not be parked suspiciously overnight. I had taken her up on the offer, surprised at her quick thinking and helpful attitude.

"What if one of the sisters asks where I am?" I asked as Madison revved the engine on her Jaguar.

"Damn, I love that sound. The low vibration of a sports car always gets me. It's like a motorboat straight to the crotch." Madison gyrated in her seat.

"Are you even listening to me?" I gripped the door handle as she backed out and flew down the street.

"Yes, I'm listening. And no one will ask. If they do, I'll just say you're staying at your parents'." Her voice trailed off. "Besides, you need some time away."

"That's thoughtful of you—and not like you. So, why are you trying to get rid of me?"

She gasped, putting her hand to her chest. "*Moi?* Get rid of you? No!"

"Okay. You only speak French when you're hiding something. What is it? We told each other, no secrets. Pretty sure that's rule number something in the BAD house. You know my biggest secret, so you can trust me."

She put her hands on the top of the steering wheel, drumming her fingertips to the radio's beat before taking a deep breath.

"Remember how I said I would do some digging?"

"Mmhmm," I hummed.

"Well, I did. And I didn't have to dig very far. I didn't dig much at all. I asked my mom."

"She knows about my family?" I asked.

"My mom? She knows everything!" She adjusted her rearview mirror, checking her reflection and making a kissy face.

"Spill the tea," I said.

My heart rate thumped in my ear, drowning out the loud vibration of her car's engine. I knew she was going to say Dominick was wanted for murder or my family had adopted me or our dads were gay lovers—which would be okay if it didn't make me and him practically stepsiblings. I cringed.

"She told me to keep my nose out of other people's business, and if I had any brain cells left after all this bleaching I'd done to my hair, I'd leave the Moretti family alone. She said they were dangerous. And that"—she hesitated—"she loves you like her own daughter, but your parents are dangerous too. I don't think she wanted me to tell you that part. She doesn't want to be involved. So, as your best friend, let's pretend I didn't say anything."

"What? My parents, dangerous?" I blew out a breath. "Only if you mean, my mom casts holy fire or my dad has unfortunate voting habits. He's old school, a boomer. His politics is as dangerous as he gets. And my mom's too church of fire and brimstone. Neither of them is dangerous." Heat rose in my cheeks as I spit out whatever I could to defend my parents.

"I know! I don't think they are either. I'm sure my mom's only heard rumors. No big deal. But she also advised leaving the Morettis alone. Maybe after this rendezvous, you two need to have a come-to-Jesus meeting. Bring your mom. Maybe she'll help." She laughed, tossing her new hair extensions behind her shoulder.

"Not even funny. But I guess everyone thinks the Morettis are some kind of criminals who will whack me for banging their son. Sheesh. In Forks?" I shook my head and stared out the window.

"Google his grandparents. His grandpa was arrested for money laundering years ago but somehow got out of it. His uncle is in jail for fraud, and he has two cousins who are awaiting trial for embezzlement. They aren't in Forks. That's upstate. And I've said too much. Your jaw is falling off." She reached over, placing her hand under my chin and gently closing my mouth.

"What the fuck? So, it's real then?" I cracked a window, in desperate need of fresh air.

"Do you think I'm making this shit up? I told you he was dangerous! Or at least, his family is! And you're about to have an overnight with a mobster! It's kinda kinky. I'm living vicariously through you. Just don't get killed." She turned the corner, pulling into the Bar Thomas parking lot.

"Gee, thanks. I might be walking into a setup. His aunt Edna probably doesn't have Alzheimer's, and she's going to gather intel and then use it against my family and me for who knows what." I motioned for her to park at the back of the empty lot.

"I promise to be your BFF and bury you in a Givenchy gown." She leaned over, hugging me, and slipped something into my hand.

"What's this?" My fingers curled around a black contraption.

"A Taser. Duh!" she said.

"Gah!" I screamed, dropping it on the console between us.

"Don't do that! You'll set it off!" She picked it back up, handing it to me. "Just point it at Dominick or whoever and push this button. I got the smallest one, so it fits in your handbag. I wanted to sew a boujee cover for it, but I ran out of time."

"You really think I'll need this?" I swallowed hard, stuffing the Taser in my purse just as Dominick pulled in beside us.

"Not for him, but maybe for that woman!"

She tipped her head toward the back of Dominick's Jeep, where a wrinkled old lady sat. She smooshed her face against the window and bared her teeth.

"Aunt Edna. She's going to kill me. I know it." I clutched my handbag to my chest.

"You'll be fine. Just have a good time and keep the Taser handy."

I opened the car door, hesitating as Aunt Edna let out a loud growl.

Dominick turned in his seat, shushing her before rolling down the window to thank Madison.

"Keep her safe," she said to Dominick, flashing him a fake smile.

"She's always safe with me." He nodded back at her.

I crawled into the passenger side and waved good-bye to my friend. But the shadow falling over her face as she pulled away told me she didn't believe him. And after the gossip she'd said to me on the drive over, I wasn't sure I did either. I folded my hands over the handbag in my lap, angling it so I'd have easy access to the weapon I hoped I wouldn't need.

DOMINICK

I knew it was probably not the smartest idea to invite Hailey along for the ride with Aunt Edna. But I desperately wanted to continue this secret love affair we had going, and to be safe, I needed to confess my sins now rather than later. I hoped I could make up for my shady history by spending alone time with her in Outer Forks on a real date without all of the watchful eyes. But after I told her what I'd done, she could disappear out of my life completely. I wouldn't blame her. A Simmons was the last person I wanted to hurt. My family had dragged them through enough drama.

"Hailey, this is Aunt Edna. Aunt Edna, this is Hailey," I said, backing out of the parking lot.

Aunt Edna reached out, grabbing a fistful of Hailey's hair and yanking. Hailey yelped, turning in her seat and shoving her hand deep inside her purse.

"Aunt Edna, no!" I pushed her hand away. The thin skin across her knuckles bunched up like crepe paper.

"Fiddlesticks! I haven't had cotton candy in years," she croaked, crossing her arms over her sunken chest.

"That's not cotton candy! That's Hailey's hair. Besides, you're diabetic. Sit back. We'll be at the doctor soon. Don't eat Hailey's hair, please."

"Nice to meet you too, Aunt Edna." Hailey managed a smile. Her eyes darted from me to Aunt Edna's reflection in the side mirror.

"Sorry. She has Alzheimer's, but she's also a little nutty." I lowered my voice.

"Who has nuts? You got peanuts? I haven't had them in years. Squirrels like nuts. You know who doesn't have nuts? Your dad." Aunt Edna slapped her knee and roared with laughter.

"She also has a mouth on her." I sighed before apologizing.

"I see." Hailey's face broke into a grin. "No worries. I'm used to mouthy BAD girls."

Aunt Edna sat back in her seat, chewing on a cuticle and spitting it out.

"Was your morning okay? Did Madison give you any trouble, sneaking away?" I clasped my hand around hers, entwining our fingers together. Every time I touched her, I felt more and more alive. Her buttery skin softening my rough edges was precisely what I needed in life.

"No, she's fine with it." Hailey smiled, relaxing her shoulders. She wedged her purse in between her door and the seat before scooting in closer to me.

"That's odd. I thought she hated me?" I asked.

"You know what I hate? Those little monkeys with the hats who steal all your money. I was rich once. Damn monkey." Aunt Edna sighed, slumping into her seat.

"Those monkeys always get me too!" I said.

Hailey put her hand over her mouth and stifled a giggle.

"Madison doesn't hate you. She just wants me to be careful. She thinks your family has mob ties. But everyone thinks that. I do need to ask you something though. When we're alone." She inclined her head toward our loony third party in the backseat.

I'd stiffened when she mentioned *mob ties* and pulled my hand from hers.

"Okay. But first, there's something I need to tell you," I said, clearing my throat.

"What is it?" Aunt Edna croaked. Her eyes fluttered shut as her head hit the headrest behind her.

"Nothing. We'll be there shortly, Aunt Edna. You should take a nap," I said.

"Squirrels do it better," she replied before rolling her head to the side and snoring.

"Is she ..." Hailey turned in her seat. "Did she just fall asleep?"

"Yep. She does that. More than a few times, I've seen her fall asleep while kneeling in church after saying her Hail Marys. I think it's part of the Alzheimer's—or it's just Aunt Edna."

"Oh. Poor thing."

"Poor nothing! She'll chew you up and spit you out in a hot minute. Which is kind of along the lines of what I'm about to tell you." I glanced in the rearview mirror, making sure my aunt was still asleep, and rubbed my slippery palm over my jeans.

"This doesn't sound like a pleasant conversation. Is this why you asked me to come with you? Because you knew I'd be trapped in a car with you without an escape? And you're about to break some terrible news to me and force me to listen?" She inched closer to her side of the car and away from me.

"Guess you've been in this situation before," I said, tightly gripping my fingers around the steering wheel.

"Go on." She lowered her voice.

I tried to keep my eyes on the road, but the sudden increase in my blood pressure had me dizzy.

"Do you remember, behind the shed, how you said you aren't sure of who you are? And you're afraid you're just who you've been raised to be? And you said you never confided that to anyone? And I told you I wouldn't tell anyone your secrets?"

"Yeah. Go on."

"I have a secret too. I'm not sure of who I am anymore either. Because I've always played the role of who I was told to be."

"Who were you told to be?"

"My dad's son. The heir to his business ... all of his businesses. Look, Hailey, I wasn't away at Welshire for school. I mean, I stayed there, but I never attended classes. I was only there on official Moretti business. My dad wanted me to take care of a few things for him, and in return, he let me come back home and go to vet school. I've never wanted any part of my dad's shady hustles. But when my dad asked me to do something, I did it. Now, I know better. I'm questioning things too."

"What do you mean, you took care of some things? What did you do? What shady deals?"

"I don't know. He refused to tell me. All I know is, I delivered duffel bags of money now and then. At least, I think it was all money—probably laundered money. The rumors are true. He's part of an old-school mob that's almost died out in Forks. But it's alive and well in other places, mainly those places he keeps traveling off to."

"So, the mob-tie rumors are true. You're really in the mob. Are you fucking kidding me?"

"No, no, no. Not me. My family. I had one little stint while away at Welshire, so I could come back home and be who I wanted to be. Everything was going fine until I met you. My dad's always been very strict about not associating with your family, but I've seen them together more than a few times."

She gasped. Her hand shot out, bracing herself against the dashboard.

"My dad and yours?" she asked.

"Yep," I replied, blowing out a long breath through my nose.

"Why? How?"

"I don't know. I think he has something on your dad. I don't know what. I'm so sorry."

"Why are you telling me all of this?" she asked.

"Because I thought I was going to be out of the woods with my family. I thought I'd broken ties and done my part. But then you came along, and my dad's asking for favors again. I think he's trying to distract me from you, which only makes me rebel more. You're something I can't have, and I don't like not getting what I want. In my blood, I'm still a Moretti."

"Yeah? Well, what're you going to do about it?" She squared her shoulders, fidgeting beside me.

"You can't just skin a squirrel, Carol!" Aunt Edna piped up from the backseat. She snarled, pulling out a gun from Hailey's purse and pointing it at me.

"Oh God!" I yelled, veering off the side of the road and stopping the car in a ditch.

Hailey screamed, unbuckling her seat belt and diving into the backseat before grabbing the gun from my aunt. But it was too late. She pulled the trigger and shot out two long wires, landing one in the back of my seat and one directly into my shoulder.

"Squeeee!" I squealed like a stuck pig.

My shoulder flexed, my arm flexed, my jaw flexed, and even my eyeball flexed as every ounce of my being involuntarily seized up, rendering me useless. I couldn't even blink to communicate what was happening to me if I tried. The blinding pain shooting through me was worse than the time I'd slipped in the gym locker room.

I'd showered with the rest of the soccer team after a game one day when some dumbass left a bar of soap on the floor. I slipped, fell, and knocked my head on the porcelain tile. I came to minutes later, surrounded by my naked teammates. Of course, John—or as I liked to secretly call him, Femur Dick—leaned down to check my pulse. He was a shower, not a grower. I wasn't checking out my friends in the shower, but some of those guys were slanging massive dongs, and it was hard not to notice. John's dick was so damn long that when he leaned over me, the tip hung down, tickling across my lashes. One quick brush of his schlong against my face and I immediately turned my head and hurled. That was my last soccer game. I'd blamed the concussion, but in reality, the blow to my ego had been much more painful.

Hailey grabbed the Taser from Aunt Edna's hands and wrestled it from her before yanking the dart out of me. I wilted against the steering wheel like a floppy fish—or a floppy Femur Dick.

"Are you okay? Dom? Answer me. I'm so sorry. How did she get this?" Hailey threw the Taser on the floorboard in front of her.

"What the fuck are you doing with a Taser?" I groaned, trying to rub the tension out of my shoulder with a shaky hand. "We could have been killed if I hadn't pulled over! I thought it was a real gun!"

"Are you blaming me for this? I didn't hand her my purse—or my Taser! I wouldn't even need the Taser if I wasn't dating a mobster!" Hailey said in a frantic rush of tears.

"Up your butt and around the corner!" Aunt Edna yelled.

"You pipe down back there and keep your hands where I can see them!" I yelled back.

Aunt Edna put her hands in the air, palms up, like she'd done it a hundred times before.

"I'm clean, Officer. I swear! I'm innocent! It's that damn monkey!" Her voice shook.

"I want to go home!" Hailey said, wiping her face. She folded her arms across her chest and strapped the seat belt across her.

"Fine! We're close to her doctor anyway. I have to drop her off and get her out of here. I'll take you straight home after." I took a deep breath and pulled back onto the road.

We drove the rest of the trip in awkward silence. Even Aunt Edna was quiet. She watched the city pass by out the window while chewing her lip and growling every so often. She probably thought she was on the way to jail. Something told me it wouldn't be the first time.

A heavy blanket of guilt weighed on my already-fucked-up shoulders. I couldn't exactly blame Hailey for protecting herself and carrying a weapon. I had a knife on me at all times. The shock—literally—of the accident and my sketchy confession had overloaded my brain, and I had reacted poorly. The truth was, when she'd asked me what I was going to do about the situation, I hadn't had an answer. All I knew was, I wanted her, and I couldn't have her. At least, not in Forks anyway.

"Hey, I'm sorry I got upset with you. I know it wasn't your fault. It looks like we're two for one now on saving each other. What's next? Are you going to save me from a vicious uncle? Because I think that one back there"—I tilted my head toward Aunt Edna—"is as vicious as my family gets. That I know of anyway. Well, except my dad," I said. I rolled my shoulder back, releasing the tension.

"It's fine," she said in a tone barely above a whisper.

"No, it's not. When a woman says *it's fine*, that's basically a death threat. I get why you have a Taser in your purse. You should. It's a dangerous world out there, and after what I just told you, it's pretty smart of you to carry something to protect yourself."

"I used to have a nutcracker in my purse. It got them every time. I'd whip it out and shake it in their face like I was about to crack some skulls. Or nuts. Your dad doesn't have any of those," Aunt Edna said, slapping her knee and laughing yet again.

I wondered if she thought that move was part of the joke.

"This has to be the oddest car ride ever," I sighed. "Let me make it up to you. Let's go to Scarlett Herb and sit down for a fancy-schmancy lunch. Then, uh, we can stroll through Outer Forks and check out the scene. It's more relaxed with a hipster vibe, unlike the uppity shit we tolerate in Forks. And if you aren't too mad at me, there's this bed-and-breakfast I found within walking distance of their square. It looked nice."

"I'll get lunch with you, but give me some time to decide on anything else. I'm still shaken up. I mean, I'm not sure I feel safe with you, knowing who you are. I thought the rumors about your family were just that—rumors." Hailey picked at a loose string on her sweater.

"My family, not me. I'm not like them, and I've tried to show you. Hell, I told you about my past because I like you. And I want you to like me too. I don't like secrets and lies. It goes hand in hand with this bullshit, elitist lifestyle I hate."

"I do like you. That's the problem. Ever since you came into my life, I've been questioning everything. I thought I was happy before you. But now, I'm more annoyed about the life I'm living. I had my head in the clouds, and you've brought me back down to earth. I never really thought about things the way you do. I was perfectly content, living in my well-financed bubble. I'm not anymore. I guess you can say, you've opened my eyes, or you've turned my entire world."

"You're such a precious thing," I replied. "Any woman who can quote a cult classic movie deserves much more than living in any kind of bubble."

"That's what they do. They feed you their lies. They twist your mind before you can think for yourself. It starts when you're born. You don't see anything, except you and the family. *La famiglia prima di tutto*. At what cost? They can dazzle you with money and fame, but behind the curtain, they're a rotting corpse with no moral compass. You follow in their steps because you were never allowed to do anything else. You can't break free. You just keep the cycle going.

You swallow it for the comfort you know. The security. All of it even if you know something's not right. Run. Run far away. Damn monkeys. They ruined my life." Aunt Edna rested her head against the window and shut her eyes.

Hailey and I looked at each other, stunned into silence. I tried to open my mouth to speak, but it was too late. I pulled into the parking lot of where I was supposed to meet my aunt's caretaker, but instead, I met my parents.

Eleven

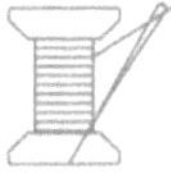

HAILEY

As soon as we arrived at our destination, Dominick's face froze in horror.

"Is that your dad's car? Didn't you say he drove an Aston Martin?" I asked, reaching back into my purse for the Taser. The tightening feeling I'd been experiencing in my chest came back full force.

"I'll handle it," Dominick said, gathering himself and pulling into an empty space away from his dad.

"What do I do? They hate me! They're going to make me walk the plank!" I glanced behind my shoulder at Aunt Edna, who was still stuttering on and on about monkeys.

"That's pirates, not mobsters. Just stay put. I'll get Aunt Edna out." He took a deep breath and stepped out of the car, winding his way around the back.

"It was good to meet you, Aunt Edna," I said, waving her good-bye.

She threw her head back and blew a breath from between her thin, lined lips. "Poof. Gone!" She cackled.

Dominick picked her up before gently setting her down on the ground. She swayed in his arms, laughing and sighing.

"Don't let those monkeys get you down," he said, patting her on the back.

She nodded, wiping her eyes.

She clung to him as they made their way across the parking lot toward Louis. Her feet shuffled three steps to Dominick's one long stride. But he waited patiently, smiling and encouraging her, even after she'd tasered him. My heart fluttered. He was too good for his family.

I shifted in my seat, wringing my hands as they inched closer to Louis. He turned off the engine and stepped outside of the car, slamming the door behind him. Even with his heeled Armani loafers, he stood almost a foot shorter than Dominick. His belly stuck out in one big roll, nearly bursting from his button-down. He stuffed his tiny fists into his pockets and fake-smiled into a sneer as Aunt Edna and Dominick approached.

I wondered how two entirely different men could be related when an older woman stepped out of the car, pulling me from my thoughts. She stood head to toe in a Mona business jacket and matching skirt. Just her suit alone cost more than my entire designer-labeled closet. She flipped her hair, took a few quick strides, and stood before Dominick and Aunt Edna with the most regal posture I'd ever seen.

She towered over Louis with the same flash of fury in her eyes displayed in Dominick's when he became upset. They were nearly identical. He was the spitting image of his mother. I'd only seen her once when I was a child, but I didn't remember her looking like the woman standing in front of me.

My pulse throbbed, echoing in my ears and sending me into sudden nausea. I cracked the window, letting the cold breeze hit me in the face while also straining to hear their conversation.

"Why are you here? I thought the caretaker was picking her up?" Dominick stiffened his shoulders.

Aunt Edna dropped her arms, leaving his side and tiptoeing to his mom.

"Things change. Your mom is taking care of her today, and I'm … I'm going to take care of you and your guest." Louis took a step toward Dominick.

My head whirled. I'd never been in the line of danger before, and after his admittance to the criminal life, I wanted nothing more than to run away. I pulled out my phone, keeping it hidden under the dash, and dialed Madison on speaker.

"Madison. Get me a ride, please. ASAP. I'm at 2011 Briar Street in Outer Forks," I spit out as soon as she answered.

"Are you okay? What's going on?" Madison asked. Her voice came out shrill and as terrified as I felt.

"No time to explain. I need a ride. Now. I can't look it up. I don't want them to see me making calls." I hung up the phone, stuffing it back into my purse while the Morettis stared each other down.

His mom put her arms around Aunt Edna and led her inside the building, never once looking my way.

"Like hell you are. I know how to take care of her. I don't need your help," Dominick said. He puffed his chest out and dug his heels in the ground.

I reached for the door handle, scanning the parking lot for an escape.

"Oh, but I think you do, son. Because you just don't listen. You know family knows best. I already have her a ride back. Much better than the silly toy you're driving. She'll get to ride home like a princess. You, you're staying here." Louis cocked his head to the side.

"I'm not leaving her. You've got to be out of your mind. I'm done with you and your business. You've already ruined her family, and now, you're trying to ruin her—and me. If you think I'm going to let you keep running all over me like this, you're wrong. Hailey's with me, and I'm with her. And we were just leaving."

The door to the building flew open, shifting their attention to Dominick's mom. She marched toward them, pointing her finger in both of their faces and yelling. Her words came out in a quick burst of English and Italian. I tried to comprehend what she'd said, but unless she'd spoken of a shriveled right boob, I had nothing.

Dominick nodded at his mom before turning and making his way back to me, pausing mid-step to let a limousine pass. Louis waved it down and jogged toward the driver. Dominick opened his car door and slipped into the Jeep, fuming with his familiar fury.

"Don't leave me," I said.

But the expression on his face told me all I needed to know. This was over.

"Don't worry, cupcake. You'll be just fine." He reached for my hand and squeezed it.

His mom had disappeared into their car, but his dad stood, staring into the Jeep. His tiny hands folded across his chest and clasped around his T. rex arms. I wanted to smack the smug look off his badly spray-tanned face and tell him he looked like a wet Cheeto in a shittily cut suit.

I tore my eyes from Louis and curled my lip. The more I looked at his face, the more pissed I grew.

"But what about you?" I asked.

"I told you, I'll handle it. I need to … take care of some things. But you aren't taking the limo back. Take my Jeep. I'll get someone to pick it up later." He pushed the key into my palm.

A fire-engine red Ferrari pulled into the parking lot, screeching to a halt beside the limousine and narrowly missing Louis. The tires squealed in a rush of smoke.

"I can take care of myself." I opened the door and jumped from my seat.

Dominick followed, rushing to my side. He stepped in front of me, blocking my way.

In the background, Louis bellowed at the Ferrari.

"Wait! Damn it, Hailey. Don't just leave like this," Dominick said.

"Why? It's clearly over. You'll always be one of them. They won't let you go. So, you have to let me go. Capeesh?" I swallowed hard and stared at the ground, scuffing my heel across the pavement.

"I don't accept that," he growled, stepping into me.

He reached for my arms, but I snatched them away. I couldn't let him touch me anymore. The longer this went on, the harder it was to leave him, and I had to leave him. There wasn't a question about it anymore. We couldn't sneak around forever.

His dad began fussing again.

"You don't have a choice. This time, I'm saving myself." I blinked back tears before pushing past him, stomping to the passenger side of Madison's ex-stepdad's Ferrari.

He was the third stepdad Madison had known and her favorite. He still visited the Sheffields often and remained supportive of Madison. But ultimately, he hadn't been good enough for her mom. No man ever was.

Dominick ran behind me, calling my name. But I opened the car door and refused to turn back. Instead, I stared straight at Louis while he stood, hunched over his belly like a greased armadillo.

"Hey, Louis!" I yelled, taking advantage of the rush of adrenaline coursing through my veins.

His dad cut his eyes to mine. His jowl sagged open as if I was crazy to even speak his name. At the moment, I was.

"Yeah, I'm talking to you, Louis Moretti. My dad says, *Fuck you, cunt!*" I flung my fingertips under my chin and shook my fist around in an attempt at a vulgar Italian gesture. I hoped it meant what I thought it meant. But knowing my luck, it probably meant I wanted to fuck his nose with a toothbrush.

"Oh my gosh," Madison's ex-stepdad, Harold, said as I settled into my seat and shut the door.

"Just go. Go! Go! Go!" I giggled in a fit of nervous laughter. I glanced in the side mirror as we pulled away.

Louis's mouth still hung open, but I caught a hint of a familiar smirk spread across Dominick's face.

"Did you just call Louis Moretti a cunt?" he asked.

"Yes, Harold, I did. So sorry I used that language! It's not like me. I just ... I've just had enough of Moretti drama!" I buckled myself in and pulled out my phone, texting Madison that I was on my way home to explain.

"You don't offend me at all! You do know I was part of the Sheffield family, right? Remember? Before she kicked me to the curb? Language like that doesn't make me squirm. Besides, did you see the look on his face? I bet plenty of people have wanted to tell him that, but you actually did. Kudos to you, kiddo. But the other man back there, was that his son?" He stepped on the gas and pulled onto the interstate, flinging us back into our seats. He was always the wild and fun ex-husband—a favorite of mine too.

"Yeah. Dominick is his name," I sighed. "He's not like them though. But he's still one of them." I rubbed my face, pushing my palms into my eye sockets to stop from crying.

"He didn't look like one of them. The way he looked at you was how I used to look at Liza. He looked proud. Some men like the *stronger woman* type. The type who can save themselves. It's a turn-on even if, ultimately, you independent women drop us like a bad habit. Though I'll be honest; I'm still a man. I love saving the day and riding in on a white horse—or red Ferrari. Whatever. I wish Liza had at least pretended to need me. Just a little. It feels good to save the girl too. It's in our nature." He tapped his fingertips across the steering wheel.

I pinched the bridge of my nose and rested back on the headrest. "I think some women just get tired of pretending."

"Yep. Not just women, but all of us. Sometimes, it's necessary. In business especially. Do you know how many colleagues I have who have the most punchable faces? But I just smile and nod anyway." He shook his head.

I pursed my lips and asked about his business, pretending to care. I wanted him to keep talking, so I didn't have to. My mind raced with thoughts of what had just happened. I needed to piece it all together before Madison barraged me with twenty questions.

My phone dinged in my purse as I braced myself to begin answering her interrogation. I buried myself in texts, nodding every so often to keep Harold talking. I told Madison everything, so when I crawled into the BAD house, I wouldn't need to speak anymore. Instead, I could drag myself to bed, pull the covers over my head, and avoid the world——at least until the stars aligned my path with a Moretti again. I shuddered at the thought.

I spent the next week in bed with my phone turned off. The only person I'd spoken to was Madison, who somehow kept me alive on iced coffees and Thai takeout. After I'd given her the rundown on my temper tantrum with Louis, she'd declared me an honorary BAD girl for the week. The other girls had no idea why they were sending me gifts and doing my chores. But Madison handled it all, per usual.

"Rise and shine, beautiful! It's my brand launch! I mean—ahem—the fashion show for charity!" Madison barged in my room and threw back the curtains. "I hope you still fit into my gear after all those spring rolls you inhaled. Now, get up!" She pulled the covers off of me and gasped.

"What?" I groaned. I threw my arm over my eyes and reached out with my other hand, attempting to find a sheet to cover back up.

"Have you even showered? I gave you those pajamas to wear three days ago! You know I let you slide on the rules this week, but this one is a stickler. You have to at least take care of yourself a little. I can't exactly put you in the shower and scrub you down. I mean"—she tapped her perfectly pointed chin—"I guess I could. Is that what I need to do?"

"No. I'm feeling better. Kind of." I pushed myself up on the bed and stretched. "Where's my phone?"

"You told me to take it, remember?" She folded the blankets and stacked them beside the doorway, where the laundry service would pick them up.

"No."

"Two days ago, when you drank an entire bottle of wine, you threw the phone at me and said, 'Don't let me touch it again.' At first, I had no idea what you were talking about. But then, I saw he had texted." She rolled her eyes. "So, I did. You'll be happy to know though that I've been keeping your social media up. Of course, I haven't posted selfies of you, but I've kept up with engagement and the odd positive mantra quote. Blah, blah."

I rubbed my eyes and leaned forward, trying to keep up, but Madison talked a mile a minute.

"Did you just say Dominick texted me?"

"Yeah. You don't remember, do you? I should have cut you off after two glasses."

"Did I text him back?" I asked.

She pulled the phone from her back pocket and tossed it beside me.

"Take a look." She plopped herself back on the bed.

I scrolled through the numerous texts I'd left unanswered and found his name.

Dominick: Hey! Are you okay? We need to talk.

Me: You R A Monkey.

Dominick: No, I don't think so. Unless we're texting about the theory of evolution, but somehow, I don't think you'd do that.

Me: Why? U think I'm sutpid? A monkey's uncle ???

Dominick: Aunt Edna, did you swipe Hailey's phone?

Me: It me.

Dominick: Aunt Edna doesn't know how to text.

Me: No! I am me. Hailey.

Dominick: Okay. Can we talk?

Me: Im not sneaking around. No moer lies. No more pretend. No monkeyss.

Dominick: Agreed.

I never answered him. A day later, he had texted again.

Dominick: Can I see you at the fashion show? It's crucial we speak in person. Please?

The last text he'd sent was a meme of the Goblin King and his giant bulge.

"What do I do?" I lifted my gaze to Madison.

She'd fallen back on the bed and stared at the ceiling while I scrolled through my phone.

"I need to tell you something," she said.

"Oh, damn. Not you too. What is it?" I turned my attention to her and braced myself. Those words set anxiety off in anyone. But hearing those words come from Madison's lips was gut-wrenching.

"You know how I talked to my mom about your ... situation?"

"Yeah."

"I think there's a third family involved."

"Who? Like someone in on the drama besides Simmons and Morettis?" I asked.

"Yes. Something like that. I'm not sure who. I don't know how you can find out. My mom mentioned hush money. I don't know if it was from your family or his or whoever this third party is. She clammed up and refused to tell me more. She knows I'd spill the tea to you."

"That's it. I'm going to ask my parents tonight. They'll be at the show. And if they can't tell me the truth, then I'm done with them."

"What do you mean, done? They're paying for your school. You can't exactly cut them off. You'll lose everything!"

"I'm in pajamas I've worn for three days. I smell like a bear that's hibernated in grease and wine. The only real part of my life I've ever felt is forbidden to associate with me. Not to mention, he's dangerous. And also, I don't like taking selfies anymore. I never have and never will!"

She gasped, rolling off the bed and hitting the floor. Her heels shot into the air before falling back down dramatically.

"Who are you, and what did you do with my sister?" she said, peeking over the mattress.

"I don't know anymore. But I have nothing to lose. I've already lost everything. This isn't me." I waved my hands around my lavish bedroom.

"Dolce and Gabbana bedsheets? A chandelier brought in from Italy? The closet full of designer labels?"

"All of it." I sighed. "Don't get me wrong. I love fashion. But I'm not happy. I feel like I'm living a lie. I need to figure out who I am. I need to get away."

"From the university?" She pouted, pulling herself back up onto the bed.

"From Forks. Maybe I can be one of those strong, independent women and learn things on my own. Break out of my basic shell."

"You know it's hard out there, don't you? How will you live?"

"I'll work," I said.

"With no experience?" She plucked a piece of lint from her sleeve.

"I'll figure it out."

"You're my best friend. I support you one hundred percent. But please don't make any rash decisions. You're so talented. You need to finish school."

"I can still be talented on my own. You don't think I could make it?" I narrowed my eyes.

"No. I know you could. But I'd hate to see you struggle." She breathed a long-drawn-out sigh.

"I'm struggling now. Just in a different way."

"Touché," she muttered.

I set my phone on the nightstand and swung my legs off the bed, forcing myself to get through the night.

"Let's rock this brand launch. I mean—ahem—fashion show," I said, putting on my best fake smile and ignoring Dominick's texts.

I snatched a flute of champagne from the tray of a passing waiter and chugged it back, watching the dozens of guests shuffling through the venue's front doors.

The Stepford women held their heads high as they crossed the threshold, wrapped in black silk and glittering jewelry. The men rested their palms on their wives' backs, parading them around the room like showpieces. No doubt to rub elbows with someone who they could use for a favor one day. They all did it. I knew because my father did it too. Countless times, we'd trudged into events none of us wanted to attend, just to show face for a future business deal.

I straightened my dress and scanned the room for Madison. She stood, mingling with Cheri and a few other sisters at the ice sculpture. Her hip jut out at her best angle, flashing the crowd a peek of her long, toned leg from beneath the slit on her dress. Even I became distracted by her naked flesh. If she wasn't into designing fashion, she could easily have a career as a supermodel.

"Champagne?" another waiter asked, lowering his tray.

"Why not?" I shrugged, taking another glass and setting my empty one on the tray.

He bowed his head and pivoted on his heels, leaving me alone again. I meandered my way through the white-clothed tables, the covered chairs, and the countless guests taking selfies together. My parents were already seated at a table nearest the runway. They were in a deep, animated conversation with two men in suits. I waited for the men to leave, so I could approach them and ask about the Morettis. It would ruin their night, but at this point, I no longer cared. I wanted the truth.

"You look divine. Hungry?" Cheri said, coming up behind me and holding out a plate of food.

"Thanks." I rubbed the back of my neck. My hair lay plastered on top of my head from an entire can of hair spray. It felt like a heavy, wet mop weighing on my shoulders. I grabbed a tiny tea sandwich from her plate and nibbled on it before washing it back with more champagne.

"Madison said we're running a little behind, but we should head back and start getting ready. They'll flash the lights soon and make everyone settle."

"Already? I haven't even had time to mingle!"

"Me neither. And this room is ripe with sugar daddies. I thought I'd bring in more work here, but I guess I'll have to wait until after I sashay it down the stage. Maybe it'll help if I throw a few smiles at 'em and flash a side boob."

"I'm glad you've found something you're passionate about, Cheri. Even if it's old men." I laughed.

"Older men are just … mmm." She licked her lips. "And there's something about being taken care of that's nice. Not because I need it, but it just feels good to be spoiled. I can't help it!"

"Nothing wrong with that if it makes you happy." I finished my drink, setting it on a nearby table.

The lights dimmed three times, signaling for everyone to finish grabbing food and get to their seats.

"Time to work." She jerked her head toward the door to the backstage dressing room.

My parents were still in deep conversation with another couple. They hadn't even noticed me.

I followed Cheri and the other sisters toward the dressing room, where Madison stood at the doorway, already barking orders. Her eyes sparkled with what I could only describe as power lust. She got this way anytime a plan of hers came into fruition.

"Hailey!" a voice called from up ahead.

I scanned the room until my eyes landed on Dominick. My breath caught in my chest as he pushed his way past guests, barreling toward me.

"I didn't say you could come! You know you can't do this!" I whispered, glancing behind me to check if my parents were paying attention. They weren't.

"I need to talk to you. It's extremely important," he said. His face flushed and glistened with a sheen of sweat.

"I have nothing to say. We can't keep doing this, so why try? I keep getting hurt over and over, Dom. Let me just live my life in my lane, and you live in yours."

"It's not about us," he spoke quickly, shifting his eyes around the room.

"Hailey Simmons! Get your butt in there and put on your sports bra and panties, pronto!" Madison put her hands on her bony hips, scowling at Dominick.

"I have to go." I dropped my gaze from his and turned to leave.

"Hey!" He lowered his voice, put his hand on my shoulder, and stopped me. "Stay away from Jen Hathaway."

"Why?" I asked.

"I solved it. I know our families' secret. Just trust me. I need to speak with you as soon as this is over. I'm waiting by the door until you come out."

"Sorry, Dominick. I need her. She's my highlight." Madison stepped in between us and shoved me toward the dressing room.

Dominick gritted his teeth, positioning himself right outside the door before Madison slammed it shut in his face.

I dragged my feet into the dressing area, passing dozens of other sisters and one scandalous Jen Hathaway. She modeled her golfing outfit in front of a mirror, smirking at her reflection. I dodged her and kept going, focusing my attention on getting through this show so I could circle back with Dominick and put our family feud to rest.

I dressed in my outfit in a cloud of confusion, anxiety, excitement, and hair spray. The BAD girls giggled, zipping each other into their outfits while Madison commanded the room.

"Hurry, ladies. I need you all to get in line according to your number. Soft sports first. We're hitting them harder as the show goes on. Remember, keep your head held high. If you fall, pick yourself back up." She stood at the steps leading to the stage and guarded the door.

I rummaged through my bag, looking for the jacket I'd stitched for Madison. I'd thought I'd have time to give it to her before the show, but things were moving a lot quicker than I'd anticipated.

"T-minus five minutes!" Madison shouted.

Cheri lined up behind Madison and adjusted her cheerleading costume. She flicked her skirt up and winked, practicing her moves to land a sugar daddy. Flirting came easy for her. Besides, half of the men in the room probably secretly subscribed to her cam show anyway.

"Looking for this?" Jen said, holding out the jacket I'd made for Madison.

"What're you doing with my jacket?" I snatched it from her hands.

"Gee. That's the thanks I get for helping a sister out. It fell on the floor. I picked it up and remembered it was yours from that day in the studio with Dominick."

"You're not a sister. You didn't make it into BAD. And my jacket was tied up in my bag. It couldn't have fallen on the floor," I said, folding the jacket and pushing it back into my bag.

Jen smirked and opened her mouth to respond, but another model whisked her away, interrupting our conversation.

I finished dressing just as the music began to play, and Madison opened the door, letting the girls file out one by one. We had fifty participants this year and estimated a thirty-minute show. But by the time we were halfway done, it had only been ten minutes.

"You ladies are walking too fast and behaving too nervous! Slow it down! We're not even in sync with the playlist! Hailey, come up here and count them in. Don't let one out before the other one has come back. I'm going to talk to the DJ and get some slower tunes." Madison rushed down from the steps and disappeared out the door.

I stepped into the doorway, peeking from behind the curtain.

"Oh, I guess I'm up next." Jen sidled up the steps, swinging her golf club. "Think I can get a hole in one?"

I rolled my eyes and nodded for her to go ahead and try.

She pranced onstage like she'd been born for this moment. I knew she was a model, but I never knew how talented she was until I saw her perform. She dazzled the crowd in a charming display of cutesy poses and twirls. She paused, sticking her golf club out at someone in the crowd. I craned my neck to see who she was pointing out and caught sight of my dad. He stared right back at her, pale-faced and clutching his chest. My mother looked equally horrified.

She gave a bow to them before skipping back to me. The crowd stood, cheering, but my parents remained fixed in their seats.

"I'd say, I knocked it out of the ballpark. Or whatever golfing term people use for winning. Home run. Hoop shot. Goal. Whatever. I don't sports." She polished her nails against her vest and continued skipping down the stairs.

Madison came back to the doorway and took my place, ushering me to the side. "Ready?"

I shook my head. I had the sudden urge to vomit.

"You're a total BADass. Now, go get 'em, tiger!" She patted my butt before shoving me onstage.

I swallowed hard and flashed a fake smile to the crowd. I catwalked my way to the end of the stage and back before I dared to look at my parents. My dad sat next to Dominick, his face boiling over in heated conversation.

I took two more steps before my vision blurred, the music muffled, and I collapsed onstage.

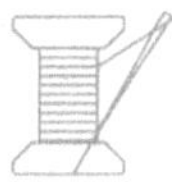

DOMINICK

"Give her some room!" I shouted, setting Hailey on a worn-out couch backstage.

The second she had stumbled, I'd rushed to her side and scooped her in my arms, just like I had that first night we met. Her head had rolled against my shoulder. She'd managed to flutter her eyes open for a quick moment before shutting them again.

"Back up! Back up!" Madison ushered the girls away. "Cheri, finish the show. Slow it way, way down. Girls, get back in line! If you're done with your part, get dressed and get out of there. We'll meet back up later."

The crowd scattered out the door, except for the few remaining models, who stood frozen in place.

"You heard the boss! Get your butts back to the stage. The show must go on!" Cheri shouted.

The girls parted, returning to their spots.

"Hailey? Hailey?" Her mom burst through the door, followed by her dad.

He took one look at me and sneered. His posture, expression, and even his mannerisms reminded me of my father.

"Mom? Dad?" Hailey croaked before becoming wide-eyed at the sight of all of us looming over her. She pushed herself up but immediately fell back again.

"You fainted. You're going to be okay, but you need some air and water," I said, fanning her face with my hand. "Don't get up."

Jen bounced over and stood beside me. "I can get it." She leaned over Hailey and brushed the hair from her face—"sister."

"Ugh," Hailey groaned, batting her hand away. "You aren't a BAD member, so you can't call me that. You're just a psycho stalker who has it out for me because I'm with him." She inclined her head toward me, easing herself back up.

"Girls, girls!" My dad put his hands up. "No need to argue. I'll call the ambulance, and they'll take care of her. Let's all get back to the evening, shall we?"

"No. I'm taking her to the hospital. She could have a concussion. Besides, she needs to get out of here." I cut my eyes to her parents, who didn't try to stop me.

Jen put her hands on her hips and stepped into Hailey's direct line of sight.

"Are you really that stupid? I'm your sister, not your stalker. Your real sister. I'm a Simmons too!" Jen hissed.

"That's enough. Come on, Hailey. You need to get to the ER." I tried to pull her to her feet, but she wiggled out of my arms.

"What? Now, you're crazier than I thought you were! I don't have a sister." Hailey blew out a wheezy breath and pushed me away.

"Yeah, you do. Ask Dad." Jen turned toward Hailey's dad and adjusted her golf cap.

"My dad?" Hailey asked.

"*Our* dad," Jen corrected her. A not-so-subtle hint of smugness escaped her smile.

"We should go, Hailey. She's not …" I looked to her parents for help, but they were as useless as I'd thought.

When I'd confronted her dad earlier, he'd denied, denied, denied. But now, there was no denying the shitstorm he'd created.

"Is it true, Dad?" Hailey whispered, rubbing the back of her head where she'd bumped it.

He opened his mouth to speak, but Jen cut him off.

"I'm not what, Dominick? Worth the trouble? Is that what your parents told you about me too? Why do you think they tried to run me off? You want to know the real reason you have drama in your families?" Jen sneered. "My dad paid your dad to keep his mouth shut about me. Yep, Hailey's dad has an illegitimate love child—me. He didn't want anyone to find out about his little mistake, and the only people who knew were the Morettis and my mom."

"Let's just stop all this right here," Hailey's dad growled.

Her mom took a step behind him.

"Oh no, you don't! I've waited my entire life for this moment. I'm not done!" Jen said, turning her attention back toward Hailey and me.

"You need to leave!" Madison interrupted her, but Jen kept going.

"Louis and his *family first* bullshit tried to talk Dad into accepting me as part of the family. But everything can be bought for a price. You know that. Dad was so terrified his perfect reputation would be put on the line that he bought off Louis with the business plans they'd developed together, giving Louis full rights. When Louis turned the business into a billionaire affair, Dad got bitter. I suspect Louis was pissed for being put in the situation and also mad at himself for taking a bribe over his own *family first* motto. So, the Simmons and Morettis hated each other. The end. You're both fucked," Jen said.

"You hid my sister from me?" Hailey planted her heels on the floor and pushed herself up, swaying on her feet.

I stood by her side, steadying her in my arms.

"I don't know what she's talking about," her dad said.

His wife buried her face in her hands and let out a sob.

"Really? Ask your mom, Hailey. She's made sure I've been as far away from you as possible. She's the one who writes the checks that appear in my account every month. She probably prays each time she writes them, that it'll be enough for me to keep my mouth shut. Or if you don't want to ask her, ask Louis. He's bound to a nondisclosure contract, so good luck with that. If he ever mentions me to anyone, his entire estate could be sued. Ah, the things people do for money! It looks like you both will lose your fame and fortune if my true identity is revealed. Hmm, what a shame that everyone in this room is listening to us." Her lips fanned out into a devilish grin.

"Mom?" Hailey's voice came out small and powerless.

"Oh, and here's your golf club back that I borrowed. I was going to wait until our usual Saturday arrangement to give them to you, but since you're here ..." Jen shrugged before handing the club to her dad.

"Why are you doing this?" Hailey asked. She bit her bottom lip to keep it from trembling.

"I was curious about you and how well you fared with our dad in your life. I wanted to walk a mile in your designer heels since, you know, you're the legitimate daughter and I'm an embarrassment to our father—someone he has to hide. I didn't plan on coming out like this, but I guess life looks much greener on your side. And that's bullshit. I have just as much of a right to live this lifestyle as you do!"

"That's enough! All of you! Look at what this has done to her! She can barely stand!" Madison unleashed the tiger Hailey had warned me about.

"Hailey and Dominick are leaving. You all sort out your own drama and leave them two alone. They're the only innocent ones out of you bunch of lunatics!" she continued.

"I'll meet you at the hospital. I'm right behind you," Madison assured Hailey, who could only give a weak nod back.

I put my arms around Hailey and carried her away, leaving her parents, Jen, and half of the BAD sorority in deafening silence.

Hailey rested her head against my car window. She barely spoke on the car ride to the hospital. I explained to her that I'd found out about Jen from Aunt Edna of all people.

I'd picked my aunt up a few days ago for another appointment and decided to grill her on the family business.

She mostly talked of animals and trees, but in one of her rare moments of clarity, she mentioned "that Simmons man's daughter." I started talking about Hailey, and she said, "No, the secret one—Jen."

I'd tried fishing for more information, but she'd only barked and snarled for the rest of the trip.

After mulling over what she'd meant by a secret daughter, it wasn't hard to guess where our family drama had stemmed from and why my parents had pried me away from both Jen and Hailey.

"Secrets and lies—the Forks' elitist way," I told Hailey.

She listened as I talked, never asking any questions. Instead, she stared into space, shutting her eyes for moments at a time. I nudged her, making sure she didn't fall asleep before getting examined. But I didn't continue the conversation. There wasn't anything left to say.

I walked her into the ER and checked her in, and before she sat down to wait, a nurse whisked her away. I sighed into my hands. We were always leaving each other.

"Where is she?" Madison marched over to me, stomping her boots on the linoleum floor.

The cold breeze blowing in with her sent a chill down my legs.

"The nurse just took her back. I think she had a panic attack," I said.

"A panic attack? Shit. It'll be worse when she gets out. Social media is already blowing up about it." She paced in front of me. Her prickly bone structure was as edgy and fierce as her attitude.

"I knew something was up with Jen. She's just so … ruthless, bitter, bitchy. Gosh, I can't believe she's my best friend's sister!" Madison plopped herself in the chair beside me.

"It doesn't surprise me. Things are beginning to make sense now." I pulled myself to my feet. "Can you stay here? I'm going to start cleaning up the aftermath as much as I can. I don't need her worrying over the drama when she needs to only worry about herself right now. If she's beginning to have panic attacks, she's going to need help. I've got some business I need to attend to. Hopefully, it'll help. I hate leaving her, but this can't wait."

"I got it. Go do what you gotta do," she said, waving me away. "And thanks. For taking care of her and keeping her safe. You know, you aren't the asshole Moretti I thought you were."

"I'm only a Moretti by blood. Don't you know? I save cats and shit." I turned on my heels to leave.

I stepped on the gas pedal and sped to the Moretti mansion, bought and paid for by hush money. I needed to get to my parents before the news reached them and they had time to think of another bullshit excuse to feed me. I didn't want any more twists or turns or lies and manipulation. I wanted the truth straight from my dad's mouth, and then I wanted out.

All of the lights in the house were on when I pulled to the front door, signaling that something was wrong. They'd left the gate unlatched, as if they expected company—me.

I only had to ring the bell twice before my mom answered. She opened the door and stepped aside, letting me push past her. Her eyes were sunken-in hollows, and her lips pressed together in one long, thin line that looked as if it had been drawn across her face with a blunt pencil. She took one look at me and turned up her palms like she'd already given up.

"Where's Dad? I need to speak to him," I asked, rubbing my aching jaw. The more pissed I became, the more I tended to grind my teeth. And after tonight, I'd surely have nothing left but nubs in my mouth.

"He's traveling," she sighed.

"Figures. You know why I'm here. You knew about Jen, and you didn't tell me," I said, throwing my hands in the air. "I thought the big secret was our mob ties and that they were somehow involved, too, because I'd seen her dad with mine! I didn't know we were under a damn confidentiality agreement not to out Jen as another Simmons heir! Now, it's obvious why you hated her. That's pretty shitty, selling your morals out for cash!'"

I blew a breath out before continuing on my rampage. My mom seemed to shrink smaller and smaller, the more I ranted.

"I knew we made shady money, but what about family first? She was a Simmons, and instead of doing the right thing, Dad accepted cash to shut up. I didn't know he could be so easily bought! Jen's a jerk. But acting like she didn't exist was wrong. And taking money for it was even worse!" I paced the floor, shaking my head in disgust.

"Look, I know you have a lot of questions. And I hate that you had to find out like this. Damn Forks. Big-city life with small-town drama. I'm sorry, son. But now, you know why I tried to scare Hailey away at Bar Thomas. She's just too dangerous to the family. Jen too. We could have lost everything if we let the cat out of the bag." She dragged her feet to the kitchen and sat down at the table.

"What? Back up. That was you in the car at Bar Thomas?" I asked, following on her heels and standing across from her. I leaned forward on the table like I was interrogating her, which wasn't a bad idea.

"It was me. You two mingling was like kindling to a fire, especially with Jen around. You know it was Jen who called me and tipped me off about you both anyway. She saw you that night. She didn't like you and Hailey together. She's a jealous one!" She chewed her lip. "I brushed her off until she threw the confidentiality agreement in my face. I moved fast after her threat. But it's pointless now. She broke the agreement, not us. We're good."

"We're not good! We were involved in this scandal, which is being blasted all over the internet as we speak. Hailey was hurt over it! Very hurt. She's in the ER!" I slammed my fist on the table.

"I heard, and I hope she's okay. I have no ill will toward her," she said, clasping her hands together and fidgeting in her seat.

"You do if you tried to ram her with the car! I can't believe you let me believe that was Dad scaring her away like some terrifying Moretti mob boss! Which is another thing we're entangled in." I blew out a breath.

"Dom, you've been a good son. I'm going to tell you this once, and we'll never speak of it again. We're part of the mob, but your dad isn't the boss. I am. I never wanted you involved in any of this, but he talked me into it. Said it would toughen up your kind heart. I tried to protect you, but I knew this world would eat you alive. You're too nice. So, I agreed to scare you a little. I set you up over at Welshire to do a few simple tasks. It wasn't even anything malicious. You were trading bags of legally obtained money, like a runner for a bank between our real business associates. I wouldn't put you in harm's way. You didn't commit any crimes."

"What? So, you're telling me, my time away was all a setup? You made me feel like I was in danger to … toughen me up? That's pretty damn twisted." I buried my head in my hands and took a deep breath. "Just when I thought the drama ended with the Simmons, now, you throw this at me. My mother, the mobster."

"You mean the world to both your dad and me. We've only always tried to protect you and put family first. If we had let out the Simmons' secret, we would have destroyed that family and ours. We also wouldn't have had all this. Call it what you will, but you've lived a good life, and you've always been taken care of with the money we swallowed to mind our own business. It's not as bad as it sounds, Dominick," she said, choking down her bullshit. Her face drooped like she'd aged ten years since the last time I saw her.

"It is to me! I don't want a part of this society that treats people like price tags. Never have, never will."

"And that's what I love so much about you. I tried to change you because I worried. But I can't change who you are. I once wanted a different life, too, but I wasn't brave enough to let my past go and take it. I kept in the familiar cycle my family had put me in, filling their roles. I'd have loved to travel the world and been a dancer. But I chose a different path, and I don't want this stressful life for you." She lifted her hip and pulled a card out of her pocket before slapping it on the table and sliding it toward me. It scratched across the table like nails on a chalkboard.

"What's this?" I asked, picking it up and inspecting it.

"Your ticket to break the cycle. This is a cruel town, and you're too good for it. At least, too good for the family stress we've put you through. No child should experience that. I've thought about this for a while, and now is the perfect time to make your getaway." She stifled a sob before clearing her throat and trying again. "You have everything you need to get started in this account, including extra money to help Hailey escape this life too. Like you told me all along, you want to save the girl. But, honey, save yourself too."

I turned the card in my palm, feeling the heaviness of a world of guilt in that tiny piece of plastic.

"Where do I go?" I lowered my voice, suddenly ashamed of my monstrous fury.

My mom was saving me after I'd completely attacked her.

"Wherever you'll be happy. Far away from the drama and into the much simpler life my son loves." Her bottom lip trembled, but she held back.

She was always the pillar of strength in our family, which now made sense. You had to be hard when you were running the local Mafia ring.

"Are you kicking me out? Will I see you and Dad again?" I felt like the small little boy who used to sit in the sunroom with her, drinking coffee and watching the sunrise.

"Of course! This isn't good-bye forever! Now, get out of here before I change my mind! Find Hailey! Find happiness! You've got my blessing. And if anyone gets in your way, you call your old mother up. I'll make sure they're taken care of." She shot a finger gun in the air and rose from the table.

I threw my arms around her, hugging her tight. All of the fight in me dissolved. The bond between mother and son was as strong as I imagined it was between fathers and daughters. I felt a pang of guilt wash over me for my family having a part in depriving Jen of that. I wondered how much her life would have been different if she'd had a loving father.

I pulled away from my mom, kissing the top of her head before turning to leave.

"*La famiglia prima di tutto*, Mama." I sniffled.

"*La famiglia prima di tutto*, son," she repeated.

HAILEY

It wasn't even twenty-four hours ago that I'd braved leaving my room for the show, and I was already hiding in it again. My parents hadn't called me to explain anything, I still hadn't heard from Dominick, and my so-called friends had only wanted more dirt to post on their social media accounts. Only Madison and Cheri had stuck by my side when I came back from the hospital.

Cheri fixed me a cup of tea, and Madison skipped any hashtagging in favor of spending the evening curled up next to me.

"I'm sorry I ruined your fashion show," I said. I sat on the common room couch with my feet tucked under me.

Madison and Cheri had cleared the room for eavesdropping ears by declaring rule number something or other: leave us the fuck alone during an emergency situation. It had a certain ring to it.

"Oh, honey, no. You didn't ruin my fashion show. Every single piece sold, and I'm back-ordered. I met my goal and then some. Your unfortunate event gave me more publicity. You know how that works. I'm just sorry it happened to you. Don't worry about me. I'm more than fine!" Madison set her wineglass on the table, put her arm around me, and snuggled up close.

Cheri's phone buzzed for the fourth time in a row.

"Shit! I got business from it too," Cheri said, rolling her eyes. "Too much business."

"You can go take care of it if you need to. I don't mind. I'll make Madison feed me cookies and rub my head until I feel better." I smiled at Cheri, who bowed graciously and ran upstairs.

"She is in her own old-geezer world." Madison laughed. "I don't see how she does it. You ever seen old-man balls? It's like two shriveled walnuts in a worn-out, old elephant trunk. Not to mention, they hang so low that I don't know how they walk! Maybe that's why older men wear tighty-whities. They need something to keep their bits from knocking against their knees."

I let out the first giggle I'd had since my car trip with Aunt Edna.

"Just so you know, I'll talk about old-man balls all night if it makes you smile like that. Or we can move to something raunchier. Ever heard of Ahegao porn? It's all the rage these days. Those girls make faces like this." Madison crossed her eyes, stuck her tongue out to the side, and drooled a little.

"No! Not Ahegao!" I laughed, nearly falling off the couch. "That's what I think Joel was into. But I couldn't make the face right. Mine was more like this." I rolled my eyes into the back of my head and opened my mouth wide.

Madison roared with laughter, standing up and sticking her hands between her legs in the pee dance. "Fuck! You're going to make me have an accident. Be right back." She held up a finger, rushing off in the direction of the bathroom.

I wiped a tear from my eye and sighed. I missed laughing and shenanigans—the way things had been before Dominick came into my life. Things had been much more comfortable then even if it was a fake life I lived. It wasn't his fault, or anyone's fault, that things had changed. The truth was bound to come out eventually. Besides, I couldn't exactly see myself as a basic bitch anymore. I was the daughter of a corrupt family with an illegitimate sister, and I had banged a mobster. My new, wild reputation almost matched Madison's—almost.

I took a sip of tea and stared into the fireplace in front of me. Rain pelted against the windows in a soggy autumn drizzle. If I wasn't so upset, this would be my ideal night. I lived for these snuggly moments and still clung to some basic-bitch tendencies.

Ding-dong.

The doorbell rang, waking me from my trance.

"I'll get it." Madison rushed back in the room, sliding on her socks across the hardwood floor. Money put her in a fun mood, and after selling out tonight, she had more than enough to put a deposit down on the boutique she wanted to open.

I swerved in my seat at the familiar sound of his steps.

"It's for you," Madison sighed. "I'm sure you two want to be alone, so I guess I'll just get the fuck out as per rule number whatever the hell I said it was."

"Thanks, Madison." I tried to give her a reassuring smile, but Dominick standing, soaking wet, on the Persian rug distracted me. His nipples poked through his white tee, and suddenly, I felt ten times better.

"You're soaked! Let me get you a towel." I rose from the couch, but he stopped me, easing me back down.

"No, don't get up. I'm fine. It's just really coming down out there. What did the doctor say? Are you okay? I'm so sorry I had to leave. I had to clear some things up. More on that later. Tell me, how are you?" His words rushed out as he sat down beside me, dripping on the couch.

"Panic attacks. She diagnosed me with anxiety. My chest has been hurting a lot lately, and I've felt faint. I never knew stress could feel like I was dying. Guess I should ease up on life a little."

He pulled me into him, tucking my head under his chin. I breathed in his scent and melted.

"I thought it might be panic attacks. I'm so, so sorry. Also, I'm wet." He held me out at arm's length. "Now, you're soaked too!"

"I don't care. I need this," I said, tucking myself back into his arms and ignoring the chill from my wet sports bra. I hadn't had time to change after the show. As soon as I had come back home, I'd crashed into the couch and refused to get up.

"Come away with me," he whispered into my hair.

"What? Like, to dinner or something? It's late! I'm not in the mood either, Dom. Look at me. My eyes are swollen from crying, I haven't washed the pounds of hair spray from my hair, and now, I'm as wet as a beaver!" I pulled back, astonished he would ask me out after a horrific night like tonight.

"No, not dinner. Forever. Or at least until you get sick of me. I'm offering you a fresh start. Let's fill these voids and get rid of the drama. Look at what it's done to you! I have everything we need, including my family's blessing—or my mom's at least. She wants me to get us both out of here."

I scrunched my brows and tilted my head, unsure if I'd heard him right.

"Did you just say, your mom wants us to run away?" I asked.

He nodded, breaking into a grin.

"That's crazy! I can't do that! What about school? And my parents? And my stalker sister? Also, I barely know you. You could take me on a hike and feed me to the wolves."

"Or I could leave you to the wolves here, cupcake." He propped his chin on his hand and flashed me the dazzling smile I couldn't resist.

"I don't know. The whole idea sounds ridiculous. No one just picks up and goes unless they're running from something or in witness protection. Are you in witness protection? Will I have to change my name to Bobby Sue?" I tucked a thick piece of sticky hair behind my ear.

He drew in a long breath. "You're much more of a Candi Carlisle."

I playfully pinched his arm, shaking my head and laughing. Candi sounced more like a name for Cheri's alter ego.

"I have school to finish, Dom," I said, slumping back into the couch.

"You know money talks at FU. The fashion academy will let you finish remotely. Your best friend's mom is the head of the place! As for everyone else, let them sort through their drama. It's physically hurting you, and you're not happy here anyway. Just take a risk and do something wild. You won't be alone. I'll be right beside you." He scooted back, edging closer to me.

"What if I end up hating you because you chew your nails or fart in your sleep?"

"Ugh!" he groaned. "Then, I'll send you back home. But this has to be a fair deal. You can't chew your nails or fart in your sleep either."

"I make no promises." I pursed my lips and stuck my chipped nails under my thighs.

"Are you still trying to find an excuse not to be stupid crazy?" he asked.

"Yes."

"Figures," he said, raking his hand through his hair. "How about this? Give me six weeks. If you aren't having the time of your life without panic attacks, I'll bring you home."

"Where do you plan on taking me? You know I don't camp or anything like that. Glamping I can do. But camping without a shower and toilet is a no-go." I folded my arms and huffed.

If this man wanted me, he'd have to learn how to handle me. I was easy, but I wasn't that easy.

"No worries, princess. We'll get a rental. But I was thinking about taking you back to the mountains nearby Yellowstone. Isn't that where you said you were happiest? There's a veterinary school there I'm sure I can transfer to. And you can finish your degree online. Build a cowboy line of hats or some shit out there."

"Do I look like I can design boots and cowboy hats to you? But maybe I could push Madison's athletic brand. Madison ... what about Madison?" I swallowed hard.

"Ah, for goodness' sake, just go!" Madison groaned from the top of the stairs.

"You've been listening this whole time!" I scolded her.

She hopped down the stairs, settling in between me and Dominick. "Of course! You know I live for this shit! What did you expect? Besides, I agree with Dom. I've noticed the change in you. As much as I hate you leaving, you're my best friend, and I'd rather see you happy. I think, after tonight, you need to take some time away. Let shit settle down here for a bit."

She smelled like she'd dipped herself in wine, which was fine by me. Drunk Madison was much more pleasant and less bossy. I wasn't sure she'd agree to me leaving her if she were stone-cold sober.

"Look, you two lovebirds, I'm not a totally selfish bitch. I know you won't be gone forever. But you don't need my permission to go, Hailey. Sometimes, to move ahead in life, you have to let go of some things, people, and ideas we have about ourselves, or else you can't move forward. And you're capable of doing very tough things. I've seen it. You're a BAD girl after all." She flicked the tip of my nose.

"You really want me to push your brand out west, don't you?" I narrowed my eyes.

"Absolutely," she said, baring a mouth full of red wine-stained teeth.

I couldn't help but laugh. I was going to miss my friend.

"I knew it!" I giggled, throwing my arms around her middle and squeezing her tight.

"Aww! Group hug!" Dominick stood up and put his lumberjack biceps around both of us in a tight grip.

"All right, all right. That's enough mushy shit for me. Ick. Let's pack your things. Do you think you can leave in the morning, so we can have one last brunch together?" Madison pouted at Dominick.

She'd tried to use the same pouty face on me once, and it hadn't worked. But for men, it was irresistible.

"Oh yeah! I have to give you something. I almost forgot. Besides, I need to speak with your mom and see if I can finish up online. Think she'll put in a good word for me?" I asked.

The sudden awareness of this dumb decision snapped me back into reality. I took a deep breath, recognizing my worry and swallowing it.

"I don't see why not. Besides, like Dominick said, money talks. Your dad would probably pay the school off to let you do whatever the hell you wanted after the shit your parents pulled tonight," Madison said.

"We should all rest anyway. You two spend tonight together. I'm going to head out. I still have to pack, too, and I need to tell Preston bye. I doubt he'll take it as well as you did though, Madison." Dominick exhaled, rubbing the back of his neck.

Madison's nose scrunched at the mention of Preston's name.

"Send him my way if he has an issue. I'll shut him up really quick." She put her hands on her bony hips and hissed.

I would have to make sure Cheri knew to hold Madison back when it came to Preston and DIK. I wouldn't be around to watch out for her recklessness anymore.

"How did someone as kindhearted as me end up with a life full of feisty tigresses?" Dominick shrugged, tightening his muscles under his wet T-shirt.

I glimpsed an outline of his perfectly chiseled chest and wanted to nuzzle myself next to it forever. Every inch of this man was anything but basic.

"You got lucky. That's how." I grinned, pushing myself off the couch and into him. I stood on my tiptoes, pursing my lips for a kiss.

"Touché," he muttered into my mouth. "Touché."

Epilogue

HAILEY
THREE MONTHS LATER

After two months of living on the road with this delicious man, we'd finally settled on a rental in Idaho. I'd never been there before, and the only thing I knew about the state was their obsession with potatoes. After my love-hate affair with carbs and my reluctance to the rustic life, I wasn't so sure about this place. But it didn't take very long for it to begin growing on me. After stumbling upon a modern cabin rental with a luxurious hot tub, I'd agreed to give it a shot. You could take the spoiled girl out of Forks, but you couldn't take all of Forks out of me.

I still read my fashion magazines and splurged now and then on a hot, new trend. But the fresh mountain air and the slow-paced small town was what I'd needed. I'd thought it would be difficult, living out of my comfort zone, but I enjoyed the challenge. Who would have thought? Life wasn't all rainbows and unicorns yet. We still depended on

Dominick's trust fund to help get us on our feet. But we were both slowly making progress.

Just this week, I'd been able to turn a profit all on my own—without the help of my parents or his. We'd both barely spoken to our families since we left Forks. My parents never explained anything to me. They instead stuck their heads in the sand and pushed money through to my account. That was how they always handled problems, and at this time, I didn't much care. I was still too hurt to mend what they'd broken, and with me gone, maybe they would have time to fix my sister and their reputation. But I knew them better than anyone, and that would likely never happen.

I focused on mending myself—with the help of Dominick, of course. I hadn't had a panic attack since that night back in my hometown. At times, I did feel anxiety lingering beneath the surface. But Dominick always stepped in, smoothing back my hair and holding me tight against his chest. He was my own personal sedative.

Once we'd settled into our new home, he'd transferred to a new veterinary school. I was also able to finish my degree, thanks to my dad's guilt money to FU. Madison's mom had had no issues convincing the board to let me virtually attend classes once she had her pockets lined yet again.

It was a win-win for everyone. I dived into my work with more energy than I'd had back when I was at FU. Dominick had even set me up a studio in the spare bedroom, complete with a sewing machine. I worked on Madison's brand a little, but I found my real passion in repurposing vintage textiles. I'd never known I could make something antique look so fabulous. These days, I exchanged my designer labels for thrifted finds—mostly.

We had no regrets about leaving our drama in the past and starting fresh, but a part of Dominick was missing. He was an animal person, and his tearful good-bye to Sanchez had even choked Madison up. When the DIK house and the BAD house had come together to send us off, saying good-bye to that mutt had been the worst part of leaving. But Sanchez belonged to the fraternity, and traveling across the country would have been rough on a dog who still ate out of golden bowls. Still, he'd mentioned his love for that dog often enough for me to cave in and buy him one.

I'd scoured the local shelter for two weeks before settling on the cutest white husky named Michael. The shelter attendant said they'd found him on the side of the road the day before, collapsed from hunger. I figured he would be not only a new friend for Dominick, but his latest project too. And naturally, I was right. He took one look at Michael and teared up. He'd nursed him to the healthy, rambunctious, and ridiculously energetic dog he was today. It hadn't taken very long. He was just a big puppy after all.

That wasn't the first time an animal had come to live with us. Dominick brought many furry friends back from school to care for them temporarily. I didn't mind. I loved to see that flashy smile of his when he snuggled them—and me.

My phone vibrated on the deck next to me right as I lowered myself into the steamy water. We used the hot tub every single night after dinner, making it a wind-down ritual. We'd sip a glass of champagne, catch up on our day, plan for our future. So far, there hadn't been any hiccups in our relationship, except one—his sleepwalking habits.

The first time I had woken to him tangoing around the room, I'd screamed and bopped him on the head with a pillow, knocking him to the floor. In my half-awake trance, I'd thought he was an intruder. He woke, crawled back into bed, and shamefully admitted his fatal flaw. I laughed and reminded him that I'd said I'd get rid of him for biting his nails or farting in his sleep. Sleepwalking was a hard pass. From that night on, we'd been barring the door with a chair. But his episodes were less and less frequent. I credited the fresh air and maybe the fact that we'd been falling in love. Sleep and life were more peaceful that way.

I sighed, rising up out of the water and reaching for my phone.

Madison's name flashed across the screen. Besides a call from Cheri or Aunt Edna now and then, my best friend was the only one I cared to hear from these days.

"So, how's life out in bumfuck nowhere?" Madison asked as soon as I answered.

"I'm sitting in a hot tub, watching the sun set over the mountains, so I'd say it's pretty good." I stood in the water, swaying my hips with the current.

"Jealous! That I could do. But being out in the middle of nowhere? I think I'll pass. I need boutiques, charity galas, champagne, and velvet! Sexy men, not rugged men."

"Ha! Yeah, you wouldn't make it then. It's a much simpler life. I'm still busy, but it's not a stressful busy, like in Forks. And I'm not in the spotlight, which is nice. I don't feel obligated to post all the damn time."

"So, what do you do? Just your work and herd cattle all day?"

"Let's see. Today, I sold eight pieces online, finished two tests, sketched a dress I'm going to work on with this new antique material I'd found, and took Michael on a nearby trail. I haven't herded any sheep or cattle yet though. Maybe, one day, we can do that together when you come for a visit. I hear cow tipping is fun!"

"Sure thing. I look good in a cowboy hat. Maybe I can lasso me a rich farmer or two. Maybe someone who owns an entire ranching estate."

"Good luck. Speaking of men, I got a hot piece of man meat coming to join me now."

I laughed as Dominick catwalked down the porch, modeling his underwear. He stuck his butt out to the left and turned to the right before slipping everything off. His cock dangled in front of me like a carrot on a stick. Again, I blamed the fresh mountain air and maybe a little bit of love for our change in silly, love-struck, or dumbstruck moods these days.

"Say hello to my thick and not-so-little friend!" He wiggled his hips before easing into the tub beside me.

"I'm going to have to call you back," I said, licking my lips.

"Wait! I need to tell you something," she sputtered, stopping me from hanging up.

"Oh no! Not again." I braced myself for whatever drama she'd bring up.

"No, it's nothing like that. I just ... well ... you know how I kept your secret?" she asked.

"Yep." I took a deep breath.

"I need you to keep mine. I have to tell someone, and you're my go-to. Between you and me, I fucked Preston," she spoke in a jumble of words.

I stumbled back in the hot tub, losing my footing and nearly going underwater. But Dominick's ever-quick reflexes caught me by the arm and pulled me back up, saving me yet again.

"You what?" I screamed into the phone.

"That's all. Enjoy your night. Ta-ta." She hung up, leaving me fuzzy and confused as ever.

"She told you about Preston, didn't she?" Dominick asked.

"You knew, and you didn't tell me?" I set my phone down and narrowed my eyes at him.

"I was coming in to tell you tonight. I only just found out. He texted me at school." He reached for my hand and pulled me toward him.

"Of course he told you! I bet everyone will know with his big mouth!" I blew out a breath, worried for my best friend.

"Probably. But I tried to talk some sense into him. It was only a matter of time for those two." He shrugged his broad shoulders.

"I can't believe it! She didn't even explain. She just hung up on me!" I rested my head back and stared up into the sky. The stars were beginning to come out. I'd never had the time to sit and look at the stars back home, and even if I had, the city lights in Forks would have blocked most of them out anyway.

Michael whined at the door from all the commotion. But after he'd jumped into the tub with us three times, we'd learned our lesson. He couldn't come outside during hot-tub time anymore. It was just too dangerous.

"Drama, drama. Let's let the kids play, and we can have adult time. You know, you're beginning to grow on me." He pulled me onto his lap.

"Oh, really now?" I laughed, straddling him. "Good. Because you're growing on me too; all of this is." I gestured toward the cabin, the mountains, the moose standing twenty feet away from us.

The moose?

"Moose!" I yelped, pointing toward the wild animal.

We froze in place and stared at our unwelcome visitor.

"Don't move," Dominick whispered. "That thing will gut us both quicker than Aunt Edna with a butcher knife."

We sat silently as the massive beast strolled down the gravel road and into the night, as if roaming the neighborhood were a regular occurrence. I wasn't sure how I felt about that. I'd need to be more careful about letting Michael out in the future.

"I've never seen anything like that! He was huge! How … incredible," I whispered, struggling to find the words for what I felt.

"That was a sign of things to come. I finally saw my moose, which means we have good luck now, right?" He scooped up handfuls of warm water, wetting the back of my cold shoulders.

"I already think I'm damn lucky." I slid myself further down into the tub and nuzzled next to his chest, tracing my fingers over the tattoos on his forearms.

"You really feel that way?" he asked, displaying that familiar grin that stopped my brain from working properly.

"Of course. I used to wake up in the middle of the night and find myself reaching out for you. I don't have to do that anymore. You saved us both from a life I hadn't even known I needed saving from. I took a risk and broke out of my basic-bitch shell. It paid off."

"Aren't you charming? I think I just made you an offer you couldn't refuse." He laughed.

"Maybe. But I have no regrets. I'd do it all over again for you, Dominick Moretti. But just you. I don't move stars for anyone." I winked.

"You're my precious thing." He pressed his lips to the top of my head and held me tight.

#blessed

THE END

Thank you for reading Dominick and Hailey's story.
I hope they left you with a world full of possibilities, a
sense of motivation, some basic-bitch love, and a tingle in
your pants. Unfortunately, they can't leave us with their
bank accounts. It's a cruel world.

If you'd like to continue with the FU series, preorder
book 2, *Sew Haute*, today and learn how Madison seduced
Preston—or was it the other way around?

Acknowledgments

For my anything-but-basic daughter, who saved me from a different life. I love you so much!!! I promise to one day get you that llama when we finally make our getaway. But you have to promise to handle the turd bombs. I'm not picking up ish.

Thank you to my mom, who continually prays for me. We both know I need it. Someone's got to save my soul after writing books like these.

And as always, thank you to my amazing editor, Jovana, and cover designer, Lori, for making my books polished and beautiful. I couldn't have stumbled upon a better team.

To my PA, Kim, you are superwoman. Thank you for keeping me on my toes and working on my never-ending task list so that I can stay writing. I couldn't survive in this business without you.

Thank you to my amazing ARC team, the DTF group, the bookstagrammars sharing the love, and my sweet author friends. Your love and support are what keeps me going. I love having you all for a supportive sisterhood. Together, we can do anything. DTF!!

And lastly, this book wouldn't have been written if I hadn't found my own Dominick Moretti to whisk me away into the mountains and show me a different side of life. So, thank you, Dustin, for your support, your kindness, your patience, and especially for your love. You've turned my entire world too. P.S. I'm still waiting on my moose.

About the Author

Kat Addams is a forever twenty-nine-year-old fashionista following her lifelong dream of writing contemporary romance inspired by the exotic men she meets in her worldly travels. At least, that's what she would like for you to think. She's certainly not a stay-at-home mom indulging in excessive daydreaming, frozen pizzas, an unhealthy addiction to purchasing pajamas, and one too many cocktails on the regular. That's some other romance author. The poor thing probably has to sneak away upstairs to write her dirty stories! What would her family think? Thankfully, that's not Kat!

Social Media:

Still crazy about Kat? Rawr! Stalk her on the social media platforms linked below!

https://linktr.ee/author_kat_addams

(For all of the links in one convenient location!)

Newsletter: https://kataddams.com/free-book

(Bonus *Hotty Toddy* Free E-Book)

Want to keep up with all the mischief and bad decisions? Be sure to subscribe to Kat's newsletter for the latest news. By becoming a subscriber, you'll be the first to know the juicy details on upcoming releases! You'll also be the first to hear of special offers, exclusive content, sneak peeks, terrible ideas, ridiculous shenanigans, and more! As a special gift for signing up, you'll also receive a free e-book, *Hotty Toddy*. Check below for more information on this stand-alone, second chance, and fake marriage novella.

Goodreads:
www.goodreads.com/author/show/
19253462.Kat_Addams

Bookbub:
www.bookbub.com/profile/kat-addams

Amazon:
http://amazon.com/author/kataddams

DTF, Dirty. Tough. Females. (A Kat
Addams Reader Group):
https://www.facebook.com/groups/
DirtyToughFemales/

(A Facebook group to stay connected,
laugh, and share. Hope to see you there!)

Facebook:
www.facebook.com/KatAddamsAuthor

Instagram:
www.instagram.com/authorkataddams

Twitter:
https://twitter.com/KatAddamsAuthor

ARC Team:
https://docs.google.com/forms/u/2/d/e
/1FAIpQLScinoImFEIChW3PQ4_BrlBo
YxpcClYTftNZRz-1DmI-
121R8A/viewform?usp=send_form

(Interested in receiving Kat Addams's
latest books before release? Click the link
to join the ARC team!)

OTHER BOOKS BY KAT ADDAMS

DIRTY SOUTH SERIES

Hotty Toddy (Free for newsletter subscribers:
https://kataddams.com/free-book)

Grit and Grind

Nashvegas Nights

Mr. Big Ego

Mayday

DTF (DIRTY. TOUGH. FEMALE.) SERIES

On the Rox

Cream-Pied

Whip It Out

Just the Tip

FU (FORKS UNIVERSITY FASHION ACADEMY) SERIES

Sew Basic

Sew Haute

Sew Knotty

PARANORMAL ROMANTIC COMEDY

Ghosted

FOR A COMPLETE LIST OF KAT ADDAMS'S BOOKS, VISIT HTTPS://KATADDAMS.COM